KT-227-764

# WE COME APART

## SARAH CROSSAN
## BRIAN CONAGHAN

### BLOOMSBURY
LONDON OXFORD NEW YORK NEW DELHI SYDNEY

Bloomsbury Publishing, London, Oxford, New York, New Delhi and Sydney

First published in Great Britain in February 2017 by Bloomsbury Publishing Plc
50 Bedford Square, London WC1B 3DP

This paperback edition published in January 2018

www.bloomsbury.com

BLOOMSBURY is a registered trademark of Bloomsbury Publishing Plc

Copyright © Brian Conaghan and Sarah Crossan 2017

The moral rights of the authors have been asserted

All rights reserved
No part of this publication may be reproduced or
transmitted by any means, electronic, mechanical, photocopying
or otherwise, without the prior permission of the publisher

A CIP catalogue record for this book is available from the British Library

ISBN 978 1 4088 7888 0

Typeset by RefineCatch Limited, Bungay, Suffolk
Printed and bound in Great Britain by CPI Group (UK) Ltd, Croydon CR0 4YY

1 3 5 7 9 10 8 6 4 2

*For Alan, Richard and Daniel – S.C.*
*For Ian and Catherine – B.C.*

PART
ONE

# Caught

You have to be quick,
none of this pretending to be browsing business
that some shoplifters go for.

It's in
            grab what you want
and out again.

But the others don't get it.
They take ages making decisions,
like they might be legit buying,
so I know before we're done
            that
we're done for.

And I'm right.

We don't make it two steps out of
Boots
before a security guard
nabs me by the hood of my jacket.
Liz and Shawna are
legging it up the high street
            and away,
while Meg and I
get dragged back into the shop
and up to an office.

'Empty your pockets,
you little scrubbers!' the security guard shouts.

'Can't make us,' I say.

'You want me to call the police?' he asks.
'That what you want?'

'No!' Meg says,
and as quick as a heartbeat
turns her coat pockets
                    inside out.

But they're empty.
No lipstick or nail varnish,
none of the mini chocolate eggs I saw her
stash away either.

'I didn't even do nothing,' she says.
She bites her bottom lip,
starts to well up.
Looks all sorts of pathetic
        really.

'Now *you*,' the security guard says,
poking the air around me with his fat finger.

I turn out my pockets
wondering if all the gear I tried to nick

will somehow disappear too,
like Meg's did.
But it doesn't.

Everything clatters to the floor:
lipstick, blusher, mascara, nail varnish
and
bloody mini chocolate eggs.

Mini chocolate eggs that *I* didn't nick.
Mini chocolate eggs that Meg can't get enough of.

She winks.
She winks to tell me to keep schtum,
to make sure I don't tell it as it is –
that she somehow managed to stuff *her* loot
into *my* pockets on the way up to the office,
that she's meant to be my mate
but is stitching me up
and letting me take the rap
for everyone else's thieving.

Again.

'What's all that?' the security guard asks,
pointing at the gear on the floor.

'Never seen it before,' I say.

'Really?' he asks.
'Well, it just came out of your pockets.'

'Can I go now?' Meg asks.

I stare at her,
hard.
Is she for real?
Like, is she actually going to leave me here
          on my own
with some mentalist security guard
and the threat of juvenile jail?

'Mum'll be expecting me,' she says.
          'I ain't nicked nothing.'

The security guard picks up the phone.
'Yeah, you can go,' he tells Meg.

Then he grins at me,
well pleased with himself –
Captain Catch-A-Thief.
'But *you*.
*You're* going down to the station.'

# HERE

In the one month
since we
arriving to live in
London North, England,
it rain most
of days,
and sunshine only a few,
which is funnier because
we come here in
summer.

Tata say we here for
short time
only
to make the Queen's cash

then

return back
to our city, town, village
for to buy:

house mansion

then

car with top speed

then

fashions for impressing

then

gifts for my older brothers and sisters
who we leave in Romania.

Tata lucky he have connections
to give him strong job.

On some days after we
arrive
I helping Tata with his
tough work.
He driving his white lorry van
around streets,
spying
seeking
searching
for the metals that people in
London North
not wanting.

We put every items on lorry and
top man pays Tata hand cash
for metals.

It good for me to helping Tata
because now I am main son
and need to
quick learn
how to make family monies
and be
provider for all.
This is what my peoples do.
Roma mens
become cash provider,
for keeping all family happy
in clothings and food.

I am fifteen
and man now,
so my working in lorry van
make much sense.

Real reason we come to
England
is because I am
older,
and cannot be without
working
wealth,
or
wife.

And Tata must to make
sacks of cash
for to pay
family
of girl
back home.

And then
we can to marry.
Which make gigantic hurt in my head.

# Caseworker

You can't even get into the youth offending services
    building
without going through
a series of locked doors
and signing yourself in with
two different doormen.

Along every corridor are
blue plastic chairs
arranged in pairs,
kids in hoodies slumped in
them so you can't see their faces.
Some of them are with their parents,
some aren't,
but there's this low rumbling
of rage in the place.

You can smell it in the air.

I don't have to wait long to meet my caseworker
– 'Dawn Green' according to her badge –
who's got the smug look of someone
who thinks
she knows
more than most people.

But Dawn Green knows jack shit
about me.

She tilts her head to one side
like she's talking to toddlers:
'So . . . taking part in a reparation scheme
would save Jess from getting
a criminal record.'

'Reparation scheme?' Mum asks.

'Yes. As this is her third offence,
the police can't turn a blind eye.
She has to show a willingness to change,
to give back to her community.'

'So it's like community service,' Mum says.

Dawn bites the insides of her lips.
'It's helping out in parks
and attending self-development sessions.'

Always quick with an apology, Mum says,
'Well, she *definitely* wants to show she's sorry.'

'And she'll do what she's told,' Terry adds,
like he's my dad
and this is any of his bloody business.

What is he even *doing* here?

'Great, so,
the police have proposed
a scheme lasting three months.
What do you think, Jess?'
Dawn turns to me,
finally,
and I know that
I'm meant to tell her
how sorry I am for being such a drain on society
and
    *of course*
I'll pick up crap down the park
to make up for it.

But a massive part of me
wants to say no,
wants to turn to Dawn and go,
*I'd rather do time*
*and get a record*
*than*
*hang out with no-hopers*
*and do-gooders*
*for the next twelve weeks.*
*Thanks all the same though.*

But I don't get a chance to speak.

Before I can open my mouth,
Terry leans forward and grabs Dawn's hand,
shakes it like they've just done a deal
and says,
'When does she start?'

# ENGLAND IS THE STRANGER
# OF PLACES

Some peoples
smile and say hello
in street or on bus.
Other peoples
not like my face
and don't returning
the smile I sharing.

Mămică feel same as me.
Sometimes I see her
feeling sad
or
I can hear her
anger conversations with Tata:

> 'This place isn't for us, they don't want our kind
>     here,' she say.
> 'We won't be here long,' Tata say.
> 'Don't make promises you can't keep.'
> 'For God's sake, Miri, we'll be home by
> Christmas.'
> 'We don't fit in here.'
> 'I know, but I'm making good money.'
> 'So when we've made enough, we'll go home?'
> 'As soon as we've the money to pay for a wife
>     and some left over.'

'Christmas?'
'Christmas.'

And I hate hearing these conversation
because many times
I not wanting to return there.
Most times
I not wanting to think about
old life.

Or
new wife.

# Bad Parent

Terry's out.
Dawn's got Mum and me
sitting at the kitchen table
with cups of tea,
pretending we're having a friendly
chat when really
she's checking I'm not living
in a shithole.
'We've got classes we can offer parents too,' she says
    to Mum,
'Empowerment for Women and other things
you might be interested in.'

Mum won't even consider it. 'Don't think so,' she
    says.

Dawn raises her eyebrows. 'We find that young
    offenders
are reacting to situations at home
when they commit crime.'

'I'm not a bad parent,' Mum says
quietly,
though she doesn't believe it.

'And no problems between you and Jess's dad?'
    Dawn asks.

'He left,' Mum tells her.

'And her stepdad?'

'He stayed.'

Dawn turns to me.
'Anything you need support with, Jess?'

'No.'

'You don't just have to pick litter
and plant flowers.
We have loads of courses you might like.'

I take Mum's lead,
shake my head
and say, 'You're all right,'
when inside
a little voice is screaming for Dawn Green
to open her eyes and figure out
who the real offender is.

# THE PETROL STATION

Every eye watch me because
one: my hair, clothes, skin, shoes
is differing from people here.

Every eye watch me because
two: I not have car, cash, friends, trust.

I walk in petrol station
to *Magic Trees* department that give cars flower
    smell,
newspapers with many hard words,
magazines with many pictures of dirty beauty girls
and
celebrities with all the sexy muscle and money.

Then I see them
close to the pay area
and near the exit get away.

I spy candy sweets.
My stomach do see-saw.
My eyes pop.

Too long since I eat
any chocolate bar,
all sitting in rows like little sparkle soldiers
making technicolour in my eye.

Which one?
Which one?
I know shop workers want to catch thief in red
    hand
so I must act
super rapido:
grab
snatch
steal
bolt.

I do the quick nab,
open door and
Usain
Bolt fast.

Security man
sprint faster.

I tumble.

Security man's big hand
dig in my shoulder.
Big carrot fingers
rip my trackie.

Tata will go off his bonkers
because he telling me many time
never let them catching you.

But they always catching me.
Three time now they catch.

That's why
I cry and have massive press in the chest.
Not because another arrest
or security man sitting his arse on me,
but because I don't want to be getting Tata's
left right
right left
jab
to the abs or head.

I see it all in my imaginings:
me on floor,
Tata snorting nose steam like bull,
Mămică helping my
tears
and
blood.

I am terror full.

That's why
I hoping police will be my protect
when Tata come get me
from
cell station.

# Good Mates

First day back at school
Liz is like,
'God, that was *so* bad.
I totally thought we were gonna get *done*.'

And Shawna goes,
'We were *so* lucky.'

And Meg's like,
'Yeah, close call, weren't it?'

I almost laugh,
not
cos anything's funny –
it's cos I can't really believe what I'm hearing.
'It's not a close call if you *actually get caught*,' I say.
   'It wasn't my first offence, was it?
And now I've got to do this stupid scheme thing,
like, every Saturday.
How fucking lucky is that?'

Meg puts her arm around my shoulder.
'Yeah . . . but . . .
what they're saying
is that only *one* of
us got caught,
innit?'

'Yeah . . . *Me*.'
Meg sighs like I'm too stupid to get her point.
'Look, Jess,
your mum doesn't
care about that stuff,
does she?
If *I* got caught,
my mum and dad would blow a nut.'

'I'm picking up shit,' I say.

Meg smiles.
'I know.
You're a well good mate, Jess.'

But I'm not.

I can't be.

If I were a *good mate*
I wouldn't be thinking about
how to get my own back on Meg.

# THREATS AND PUNISHMENT

After my arresting
they threatening me with young people jail.
They tell me I'll be *bitch boy*.
'Look at you,
all dark skin,
dark eyes.
It'll be a bit of exotic for them,' Security Man One
     say.
'They'll be gagging to get their hands on you,'
     Security Man Two say.
'Good looking lad like yourself,' One say.
'Foreign,' Two say.
'Pretty boy.'
'Fun boy.'
'Lovely.'
'Bit of crumpet.'
They scare me too much with bitch boy story
so that I tell to them all truths about my
steal.

But when real police come
they not send me to
young people jail.

For goodness gracious sake no.

They send me to something called
'reparation scheme',
head down,
tongue shut
with other
terrible teenagers.
They also tell Mămică and Tata that I must go to
    school
because 'as parents' they have a
    'Duty of Care'
and
    if we are living in this country
our family
    'must adhere to the laws and rules in England.'
They say at end:
    'Is that clear? Got it?'
If not *got it* Tata must go to man jail
or pay heavy cash fine.
And who will be the blame?
Me, that's who,
    like all other times.

School!

Night . . . mare.

# Just in Case

I've been stealing stuff for ages.
Can't remember the first time any more,
but it was way before
I started secondary school.

Small stuff back then —
　　　　other kids' rulers,
　　　　fags from Mum's bag.


And I hang on to loads of the stuff I've nicked,
not because I'm one of those freaky hoarders
you see on TV
or anything.
It's cos I don't steal stuff you can sell,
nothing of any value:
I mean,
who wants to buy a pair of Top Shop tights,
cheap mascara,
gloopy nail varnish
or pencils pinched from a teacher's desk?


I take the gear out now and then,
and I
can't help feeling proud of all the times I got away
　　with it
before they finally caught me. . .

then caught me again and again
      and gave me my very own caseworker.

There's a knock on the door,
and before I can throw everything back into the
   shoebox,
Mum's in my room.
'I got KFC for dinner,' she says,
      then stops,
      stares at the stuff
      piled on the bed,
      frowns.
'What's all that?'

'Just some things I found,' I say.
I chuck the stuff back into the box,
push it underneath the bed.

She rubs her forehead,
letting a load of worry trickle into her face.

Thing is,
*that's* not the box she should be worried about.

See,
I've got a different one on top of my wardrobe.
I've got a box filled with supplies:
a toothbrush, tampons, spare T-shirt, socks, knickers

and a couple of crisp fivers
just in case.

Like,
just in case,
    I ever need to get out of this place

    in a hurry.

# HIGH VIS

At reparation scheme
they make me dress in
high vis vest
in piping hot park.

Me and many criminal others
cleaning muck,
sweeping leaves,
picking up, picking up, picking up
crisp packet,
fizz can,
half kebab,
booze glass,
butt cigarettes.

The lives of the pollute people.

# Breathing Down our Necks

Mum and I are watching
*Jeremy Kyle*
which
makes me feel way better about my life,
looking at a bunch of losers
and knowing that no matter how
horrible everything is for *me*,
I'm not
      *them*;
I'm not in the gutter just yet.


'Shouldn't you be picking litter, Jess?' Terry asks.
He cracks his knuckles
because he can.


'Just Saturdays, isn't it, Jess?' Mum blurts out.


Terry leans on the doorframe,
sniffs
and sips at his can of beer.
'But did I ask you, Louise?' he says.


'Sorry,' Mum whispers.
She turns off the TV,
jumps up from the couch
and scurries into the kitchen.
'I better get started on dinner.'

Terry peers down at me.
'You know,
getting into trouble at school is one thing,
but having the police breathing down our
    necks
is something else.
I don't like it.'

I nod.
'I know.
You already told me, Terry.'

He sniffs hard.
'You being cheeky?' he asks.
He cracks his knuckles again.

Mum is standing behind him,
shaking her head,
her eyes wide and terrified
cos she knows that if I do anything
to annoy him,
*she'll* be on the receiving end of his boot.

'No, Terry. Sorry,' I say.

I go to my room,
curl up on my bed
and wish it weren't Monday,
wish I were

picking litter instead of here
in this house,

with
him.

# PERSONAL DEVELOPMENT

Some Saturdays we do the job
of servant men,
when body sweats and hand sores
with hurting.
They calling this 'Personal Development'.

'Personal Development' help everybody to
   becoming
decent peoples again.

In park
I am part of team,
but not the same like
when I was strong member of
wrestling team in my village.
In park I am not
captain;
here I am in
Offenders Boy Team.

One Saturday
ex-Army man, Bicep Andy,
take my team to pond,
shows us giant bag of plastic,
many woods and strings.
  'Right, lads, your task is to use only
the wood, string and plastic bottles

to build a raft.'
All faces confusing.
Much puffing of air.
   'A raft?'
'Yes, Lee, a raft,' Bicep Andy say.
   'What for?' other guy say.
'Well, Rick, it'll improve your
communication and collaboration skills.'
Bicep Andy tap Rick on back.
   'Doubt it,' Lee say.
'Your raft needs to take one member of your group
from this side of the pond to the other.'
Bicep Andy point to other side,
where girl team make also.
   'Whatever,' Bill say.


I tying strings
tighter,
better.
Rick and Lee do
design control and
building of square boat.
   'Right mate, hop on,' Bill telling to me.
And I thinking:
I could show him my skill.
Grab
flip
hold.
Learn him the respect.

But this would be very bad communications.

I jump on tiny boat.

It not float.

# Faffing Around

It's like these caseworkers pull ideas
out of their arses
and all agree
it'll do us the world of good.

This morning I'm sitting with the other girls
whinging about
how tough it
is to be female.
Dawn reminds us
how important school is –
'And I don't mean sitting in the inclusion unit,
    girls!'

And now here we are,
up against the boys,
but on the other side of the pond from them,
faffing around with
rope and wood
and arguing about which one of us
has to sit on the stupid raft we're building
once it's in the water.

Fiona goes, 'You ain't getting me on the *Titanic*.'
Jade is like, 'The raft's tiny, you moron.'
Fiona goes, 'Whatevs. I ain't doing a DiCaprio,
    right.'

And Jade is like, 'Well, I got my period, innit. I
    can't go swimming.'

Dawn sighs. 'The key is cooperation.'

Fiona rolls her eyes. 'Yeah, right.'
Jade crosses her arms over her chest.
'You know what, Dawn,
I reckon health and safety would
be all over this raft-building bullshit.'

'*I'll* do it,' I say, just to shut them up.

From the other side of the pond
come hoots
and whistles.

'He got soaked, man!' Rick shouts.

One of the boys is in the water,
his head bobbing up and down
like a beach ball.

When he comes up he shakes his hair out
like a dog,
laughs
and splashes the other boys on the bank
as though it's nothing at all
to have fallen into the pond.

'Who's that?' I ask Dawn.

'That's Nicu,' she says.
'Good egg, that one.'

# WOMAN LONGING

Mămică tears because she missing her other
   childrens.
Daughters
back in village with tiny babies,
sons being mans of house.

I wanting to give Mămică my
super son hug,
for remember her that she have me,
her very own younger boy,
in this country.

But I am older now for
super son hug.
I watching her at table
with photos,
with tears,
with suffer.

Always she saying same thing:
'I want all my babies in one place.'

Always she talking of return to our village;
'I want to go home to Pata.'

That is why I only looking,
not speaking,

caressing her tearing
or
soothing her feeling.
Mămică not want to listen to
*my* need.

That one day my whole family can come to
visit
 here.
        Live
        here.
        Working
        here.

In my new country.

# When Liam Left

Liam just left.

I woke up one morning,
saw his bedroom door was open,
but not him in among the squalor
with his
bare legs dangling out of the
        side of the single bed.

'Where's Liam?' I asked Mum.

'Gone.'

'Good riddance,' Terry said,
and I had to bite both my lips
really hard
to stop myself from saying something
like
*Yeah,* you *did this, Terry.*

Then
I left for school like normal
but didn't go in,
hid between
the recycling bins
in the Queen's Head car park.

And I couldn't stop crying,
couldn't even breathe properly,
because without Liam
I was on my own.

Completely and utterly
on
my
own.

# LANGUAGE

When I hearing this
fresh English language,
I think I will be
able
never
to speaking in same tongue,
to telling my joke
or
showing my imaginings
or
being the great listening ears to peoples.

But.

English is the tough watermelon to crack,
a strange language with many weird wordings:
*heart in your mouth*
*fall off the back of a lorry*
*if you pardon my French*
and
too many more.

We have ways to understanding though:
Michael Jackson helping Tata with learning.
Celine Dion helping Mămică with learning.
YouTube and Jay Z helping me.
*Breaking Bad* helping everyone.

43

I working hardest than ever
to being in this England world
fluently.

I not wanting to
start school
with too much
foreign tongue.

# Recording

Terry stands in front of the TV even
though I'm watching it.
I don't shout, 'Get out of my bloody way, Terry!'
I say sweetly, 'You all right, Terry?'

He holds out his phone
and I go cold,
look around for Mum.

'Film me
doing my press-ups,' he says.

He pulls off his vest.
I take the phone.
'Why?'

'I wanna examine my technique,
you know?'
He flexes his muscles.
Rolls his neck.

I press the red button,
watch him as he hits the floor
and counts to fifty,
each press-up punctuated by a grunt:
'One, *argh*, two, *urgh*, three, *huuu*, four . . .'

By the time he's finished
his face is as red as a battered pizza.
He stands up all sweaty and panting,
pleased with himself.

'How did I look?' he asks.

'You looked *great*, Terry,' Mum says.
She's wearing a bathrobe,
her hair hidden beneath a towel.

Terry snatches his phone from me.
'Make me a cup of tea, Louise,' he says,
and falling down into an armchair,
turns the TV off
and watches himself
puff and pant
all over again,
with an ugly
grin on his face.

# NASTY WEATHER

My clothes is heavy with raining.
My feet squash and slip
in my shoes.
My hair stick to me like I step out of
deep blue sea.

In England it rain
all times.

Reparation scheme is zero happy when wet.
Every other delinquents
shielding under shed hut,
smoking, spitting, stone kicking,
bantering.

All delinquents except two:
me
and
girl.

Not us.

I am under umbrella tree.
Girl hide below kids' silver sliding tube.
She seem lonely.
She seem lost.
She seem total tragic sad.

And I want to rush to her feelings,
show her my smiles,
make conversation chit-chat,
peace her mind.

Maybe tell some tale of my land,
how stars shine so bright,
how wild horse tame with one kind hand.

But
for this girl of perfect visions
I remaining under umbrella tree
and follow only with my eye.

# Eyes

I know he's watching —
Nicu,
the boy who fell in the pond
and didn't moan about it.

But
what docs he see when he looks at me?

What does anyone ever
see?

# BAD SHOES

So we go to garment shop to get
a tie,
grey shirt,
clunk shoes,
and I ready for going to school.
It feel like I dressing for wedding,
and I wonder
how everyone put on these elegants all days.
School in England must be like
big song and dance
or
the military with these uniform.
Students all looking same.
And I hoping
it be more easy
now
to be one of them.

School happens on
Monday
Tuesday
Wednesday
Friday
and
Thursday.
Phew!

School and reparation scheme my new life,
but I still don't miss my old –
no way.
Never going back,
where people like us
always
under attack
from the rich-wealthy and those born of plenty.
Here
everyone is Romanian in all eyes,
but
back home
we are the Romani Roma gypsies
and we are kept in gutter.

No chance.

Here
with school, reparation scheme
and bad shoes is better.

Safer and sounder.

# Pretty Good

It's weird
cos
I thought that
getting nicked
would be one hundred per cent
horrendous.
And I guess it is at home,
with Terry going on about it all the time
and Mum tearful.


But at school it's not like that.


At school
everyone looks at me
like I'm some big celebrity.
And since I started the scheme,
I haven't had to queue for lunch
          once.


It's like they're all afraid of me.


Like getting in trouble with the police
is a shield –
  or a weapon.


And it actually feels
pretty good.

# OLD HOME

Back in Pata, in my bed,
I listen to the
*Tip . . . tap . . . tip . . .*
On the old house tin roof.
Every night I listen to these sounds.
Sometimes when raining is too much,
the
*tip . . . tap . . . tip . . .*
fall on my head, nose, cheek,
tongue.
Fresh clean water in my mouth,
falling from our sky,
which is better than the muck water that
fall from our filth tap.

The toughest of times.

Winter hurt our bones.
Summer hurt our skins.
No money hurt our bellies.

Tata say political man
    not give a shit about us.
They give:
no road,
no light,
no house.

Mămică say they treat us
    like the world's disease.
They take:
our land,
our dignity,
our choice.


Here is decent good.


But sometimes,
when I look from window
or
go for long street walk,
I see something same between
old village then
and
new place now.


Many peoples with much miserable in their heart,
many peoples with little monies,
all walking
up down
down up
stopping
starting
again
again,
smoking in huddle group
and

chatting in small circle.
Everyone watching everyone do same things.
Peoples with no place to go for laughing and be
    happy.
    Same as my old village.
The atmospheres, buildings and peoples
in London North
is like giant rainbow.
But
not beautiful colours
    with golden treasure at end.
Is the rainbow with
white to grey to brown to black.

Sometime when I walking past
high sky houses,
I thinking that maybe some
politician take also:
land,
dignity,
choice
of these London North souls.

# Arse

We're not long back at school
before
I'm thrown into inclusion
for telling my form teacher
to kiss my arse.

      It was a joke.

And
like I'd let her near my arse.

What the hell is her problem?

# WELCOME

The lady teacher
give no smiles.
She keep everything serious.
I think maybe her man go with too much women
or
someone die in her family.

*Then* I understanding:

Lady teacher is angry annoyed with *me*.
Her boobs expanding.
She is full with irritating.
'Your name?'
'Nicu Gabor,' I soft say.
She huff like wolf.
'Right. OK.'

She writing and move paper on table.
'I doubt you'll be able to catch up.'
Her voice turn to whisper,
    'Just keep your
head down and behave.'

Her eye go to my eye.
She say, 'OK . . . erm . . .?' fighting for find my
    name.
I don't tell her again.

She point her finger to chair.
'Right, sit there for now. But when the others get
   here
you'll need to find somewhere else to put yourself.'
I walk to chair
without giving lady teacher
my smile,
my thank you.

# That Bird

We sit in the Sainsbury's car park passing a bottle
of cider around.
Meg acts like she's pissed before she's even had a sip,
and once she's had a few mouthfuls
she flaps about and asks Dan who he fancies,

hoping he'll say her,

which he doesn't.

'Know that bird in lower sixth
with the massive tits?' he asks.

Kenny laughs.
Ryan snorts.
Meg tries to look interested.

'There are like a hundred girls in the sixth form,'
I say.
Dan looks at me,
         down at my chest,
and I wish I hadn't opened my mouth.

He smirks.
'Nah,
but there's this one bird
and she's pure porn material.'

His mates laugh again.
Shawna swigs at the cider.
Liz looks at her phone.
'What a whore,' Meg says.

'Here's hoping,' Dan says,
hooting,
high-fiving his mates
then
grabbing his crotch and squeezing it.

Like anyone wants to see *that*.

# FIRST WEEKS

Things no one do on first weeks:
say hellos,
give smiles at me,
say sorry when chucking pens . . . and other stuffs,
understand my confusing,
show me the way for doing lessons,
ask me to joining in with their fun times
and
be friendliness.

Things I do on first weeks:
say my morning, afternoon hellos and goodbyes,
give smiles at all teacher,
try harder for to become part of England,
say sorry when they shoulder bump,
hide when I hearing big laughs close by,
look out of window because no one explaining
    school education to me
and
close eyes for wishing new life get better.

# These Sessions

Dawn drags her chair so close to mine
our knees touch.
'So, Jess,
how are things going?'

I open the App Store on my phone
to look for updates.

Dawn's proper pissed off.
She breathes loudly through her nose.
'You have to take this seriously.'

'Do I?'

Dawn puts down her clipboard
and sits up straighter.
'This is about your future, Jess.'

Yeah, great.
Whatever.
I mean,
what sort of future can I have with Terry around?
Cos he's furniture now.
And as immovable as wallpaper.

'Everyone takes part in these sessions,' Dawn says.

'What, even the one who doesn't speak English?'

'Even him.'
I roll my eyes to
show Dawn how boring this is.

I'm not like that guy, Nicu.
I can't get excited about
raking leaves
and doing all that self-esteem rubbish.

I can't put on a brave face and pretend that
at the end of this
things will be different.

Maybe for him they will be.

But for me
they won't.

Nothing's ever going to change.

PART
TWO

# WORSE THAN DEATH

At school I am
the boy worse than death.
Me,
the boy people won't waste breath on.

Teacher puts me in no-hope group.

No-hope group is for kids who don't know
numbers,
words,
history,
science,
facts,
neat writing,
behaving,
more.

I do know things.
But teachers never question,
they never ask.

But
I know many things:
books,
music,
ideas,
horses,

more.

      Even much English in my head
but
not so well out of my mouth
yet.


Teachers not care because
they only see disorder not student.
Also
I almost went to young people's jail,
      so I always criminal.

# The Half of It

Mr Morgan passes out the test
and tells us to sit as
        far apart
from one another as possible.

Suits me.

Then he says,
        'You may look up for inspiration,
        down in desperation,
        but *never* side to side for information.'
He laughs at his own hilarious joke
like we haven't heard it
a hundred times already.

Meg smiles at me and rolls her eyes
like she couldn't care less what Morgan says,
but as soon as the test is slapped down on to her
    desk
she goes white
and gets scribbling.

I look at the numbers and letters,
maths that might as well be Chinese,
and spend the rest of the lesson
doodling in the margins –
messy circles mostly.

Morgan collects the tests,
looks at mine:
first name at the top
followed by empty boxes
meant for answers.
He winces
and
when the bell rings, asks to see me,
and comes so close
I can see his nose hair.

'You're a smart girl,' he says,
which is a lie.
It's what all the do-good teachers say:
*you could be anything,*
*you could go anywhere.*
*Try really hard*
*and all your dreams will come true.*
But we aren't in Disneyland, are we?
And anyway,
          what could any of them know about our
     dreams?
I bet they don't live on grey estates and
eat Mars Bars for breakfast.

His eyes glint with delight,
like he's about to bag a big secret.
'I hear you've been in trouble with the police,'
he says.

'Sorry, sir, but what has this got to do
with algebra?'

'Just wondering if everything's OK.
You used to be good at maths.
If I knew what was happening, maybe I could help
get you back on track,' he says.

Just then I spot Meg standing by the door, listening.
I stand up and
push the desk away,
give Morgan the look I usually save for Terry
when he isn't looking
and say,
'You think I care about maths?
You don't know the half of it, sir.'

# COOL NAME

The girl from reparation scheme,
I see her in school.

My heart rat–rat–rattles.

    Does she see me?

We never speaking to each other.
Today is day we do?
I put loose books in bag,
hide behind locker row.
I watch.
Imagine.
Dream.

She's never said
*hello.*
*Good morning.*
*How are you?*

But I swearing my heart is in her mouth
when I seeing her.
I dreaming of chat introduction:
    *'Hi, my name's Nicu.'*
    *'Nicu, that's a cool name.'*
    *'You thinking?'*
    *'Totally.'*

I'd like to have the *cool* name.
Me,
Nicu,
the boy with the cool name.

# The Girl with the Camera

Terry makes me hold the phone
and record every moment of him
beating the crap out of her.
That's my job,
though I never applied for it.

I *could* throw it at him.
I mean,
I could use the phone to crack his skull open,
smash his brains to bits,
instead of recording what he's doing –
beating Mum
with such steam
you'd think it was an Olympic sport he was
     training for.

I gag
a little bit
whenever he glances into the lens.
Or maybe he's looking at me,
making sure I *am*
     holding the phone steady,
doing my job.

I don't want to let him down,
or I can guess what'll happen:
it'll be my belly under his foot,

my face against his fist.
Or worse,
Mum'll get it again.

Afterwards he goes out,
    down the pub
    to his mates,
who all think he's a right laugh,
        a right geezer
for having a bird who cooks and cleans,
wipes his arse
if he asks her to.

And Mum?
She heads for the bathroom,
locks the door and cleans herself up,
then into the bedroom where she
covers the bruises with a turtleneck and too much
    foundation.

That'll make him mad too.
Can't she learn a lesson?

When she comes into the kitchen
I'm sitting there
at the table,
pretending to finish off my French homework,
verbs drills,
lists of words

that start the same
but end
        differently
depending on who's doing the talking.
And I wonder whether my life could be like verb
    endings,
whether things here would be better if Mum
    weren't such a
wimp all the time.
Like,
if she was someone braver,
would Terry give up and go away
and hurt someone else instead?
Would we get to have happy endings
sometimes
instead of a constant stream of shit?

'You want some toast? Cereal?' she asks,
really gently,
and I hug her,
scared it'll hurt her,
but so sorry for not stopping Terry.

# WHO I AM

When I watching television movies
all actors
speak too speedy
for my comprehendings,
and I thinking
it be mission impossible
to learn this language
with fluent.

It so much frustrating
when words can't escape my head,
when peoples not
understand my meanings.
All I want
is for them to see how
I am fun,
clever
and
nice guy.

I afraid no one
ever know who I am.

# On the Rob

Mum sighs and lights a fag.
'This is the end of the trouble, Jess,
innit?
I don't think I could take another
incident.'

'I'm late,' I say,
which isn't an answer,
but I can't promise I'll be good for ever,
and she knows that.

When her back is turned
to the toaster,
I rob a few fags from the freshly opened packet
and have one lit before I'm out the door.

And then I'm inhaling
great gulps,
like it's oxygen,
like I've never had a smoke before,
and by the time I reach the youth offending
    centre
I've finished off all three,
and I've got nothing to do except
pick actual litter.

Dawn
sort of smiles at me when I arrive,
like we might be friends.

But she hasn't got a clue who
she's dealing with.

And
she doesn't know it was Rick who keyed her car
    last week,
and Fiona who nicked her phone.
She's so gullible,
thinks she's helping to
reform,
rehabilitate,
reissue us into society,
all scrubbed clean and ready to make nice.

The only one she can probably trust is
Nicu.
He's the one we all avoid.
Can't understand much anyway.

And he's weird.

An immigrant gypsy boy
who looks half-wolf
if you ask me,
picking litter and leaves like it's cash,
greedy for it.

'You want my helping you?'
he asks today,
trying to team up
before I've even had a chance to get my gloves on,
and I sneer
as best I can.
Sneer at him
and his bullshit English.

Gypsy wolf boy.

# A BUCKET OF SPANNERS

Everyone laugh and make jokes.

I stay far,
picking
dead leaf,
cut grass,
pongy food,
sharp glass.
Many caseworkers never speaking to me.
They just wave and point to filth I should see.
'Understand?'
I nod my head
Yes, I understand.
I'm not the real no-hope.

Lady Dawn swings her flower dress around her
    bum and
hums tunes.
I think she is liking me.
She not believe I am wild animal
        like other delinquents.
Because
I not wild animal.
I am pussy cat.

I come out from massive tree,
do the baby step to go nearer to girl from my school.

She stands not with the others.
No laughing or making joke.
Her eyes on ground
in deep thinkings.
She look depressing,
eyes all puffy red.

Her sack is empty
of rubbish.
Dawn can add days if we are lazy dogs,
if we don't helping our community.

Maybe she need my rescue.
A friend.
A man for muscle work.

My baby stepping bring me metres from her.
Two red eyes flick up to me.
I shine my smile.
She sniff hard.
Empty sack is no good.
    'You want my helping you?' I ask.
She look in air
and does a snigger laugh,
which is good because
laughing is the medicine for not being sad.
'You talking to me?' she say.
'I talk yes.'

'What do you want?'

'You want some my leaves?'

'No thanks, creep.'

I not know *creep*, but her voice tell me it's same as

dick

knob

wanker

prick.


'I am Nicu.'

         I say my name to show my friendly.

'I *know* who you are.'

'And your name, please?'

'*Nicu*, what sort of name is that?'

'I from Romania,' I say.

'Romania! Long way from home.'

I do laugh because I *am* long way.

She do laugh from belly also.


She ask me for cigarette,

I tell her no way because I not

want to die.

She do more laughing.

'You're as weird as a bucket of spanners.'

I pretend I know her meaning.


I want to tell her how much beautiful she is,

not like village girls

Tata wanting me to marry.

Sorry, not *wanting*.

*Forcing.*

# Vermin

Terry's in a top mood,
frying up pancakes
and whistling like a postman.
But I don't ask what's got into him,
what the good mood's for,
cos that would be
stupid.

And there's
no reason why anyway.
Never any reasons.
Not real ones.
Not ones to hang your coat on.

'Hey, nip down the shops and get us a little bottle
    of lemon juice,' he says,
all cheerful,
and slides a fiver across the countertop
with a wink.
A wink
and a smile,
like a real dad.

The bastard.

I take the cash and go to the corner shop.
The old guy knows me there,

keeps two bald, beady eyes on me.
Like I'd nick anything
with him watching.
In broad daylight.
Cameras everywhere.
I might be a thief, but I'm not a moron.

On my way home, I stop by the park.
Not to litter pick,
just to have a smoke
without Terry finding out
and giving Mum a clattering for not
taking better control of me.

It's empty,
the park.

Quiet.

I sit at the top of the slide
and puff away
when wolf boy appears
out of nowhere,
climbs up next to me,
hands over his bag of pick 'n' mix –
cola bottles,
chewy fried eggs,
sweet 'n' sour snakes.
'Will kill you more slower,' he says,

grabbing my fag and firing it down the slide.
'Oi, you're paying for that,' I say.
'Paying where?' he asks,
cos he doesn't really understand much.

Not words anyway.

But he says,
'Life shit pile today?'
And I laugh.
'A right shit pile every day, Nicu.'

# BYE BYE BAD BOY

The jelly egg and sugar snake sweets
I eat
make my nerves better,
giving my heart a break.

And I smile when I spy her,
high on kids' sliding tube,
smoke up in the air, puffing from her head.
That girl has to know cigarettes make her dead.

I do the sneak walk,
like a spy.
I'm behind her.
I act like flash man.
I flick her fag down tube,
offer her a sugar snake.
'Will kill you more slower,' I say.
I become brave and sit beside.
Again I see her sad eyes.
    'Life is shit pile today?' I ask.

She laughs.
        Hip hip hooray!

'A shit pile every day, Nicu,' she say.
I laugh also
and feel warm because she speak my name.

It sound weird coming out her mouth,
lovely weird,
make-my-stomach-tickle-weird.
   'Snap!' I say, because our living is the same.
   'Snap? What you on about?' she say,
with trouble eyes,
but eyes anyway that could be on a Christmas tree,
twinkling
twinkling
        brightly.

I look.

# Secrets Shared

He acts as though secrets can be shared like sweets.

But I hardly know him.
Not sure I can trust him.

I mean, I don't trust anyone,
usually,
and definitely not with stuff about *him:*

Terry the terrible.
Terry the terrier.
Terry the twat.

'You can talking with me,' Nicu says.

And for some reason
I know he'll be good at keeping secrets
so I start to speak.

But I can't tell him everything.

# STRUGGLINGS

'Jess,' I say.
'What?' she say.
'My life too has strugglings every day.'
'Really?'
'Big strugglings.'
'Sorry to hear that, Nicu.'
'Thank you.'

We laugh in same time.

'My family too is arse pain,' I say.
'Yeah, but I bet you don't wish any of them were
    dead.'

We look
to each other.

# Breakfast

Terry's pancakes are cold
and his mood has cooled down too.
'What took you so long?' he asks,
but I can't say
*Nicu,*
can I?
*Nicu? he'd say.*
*Sounds foreign. Is he foreign?*
*Thought we'd voted them all out.*
*Dirty immigrants.*
*Rat scum.*
*Knock those boats outta the water before*
*they arrive, I reckon.*


So I say,
'They didn't have any lemon juice.
I had to walk to the Co-op.
Took me ages.'
But it doesn't matter what I say now.
I've riled him.

'Louise!' he shouts.

# GOOD CITIZEN

Even though we here in this country,
Tata think for ever of home,
his peoples,
his cultures,
of village with no road or toilet.
Every day he talk of return,
always of the past.
'As soon as we find enough money for a wife,
we'll go back,' he say.

I wanting to
remain:

learn my English,
be the good citizen – no more thief,
wave bye-bye
        to bad boy.

When day come to return home
to meet wife from village,
I will cry.
I will hide.
I will disappear like magic.
Lots of cash
Tata say
he have to pay,
for finding me honest wife.

But
I am not the cow on market day.
'I want to stay here!'
I tell to Tata in high voice.
I need to
go to school,
work the hardest,
have a job like businessman, making clean money,
find my own wife.

Tata puts finger in my face.
He screaming with the loud mouth:
'You're going.
    You do what I tell you to do
    and that's the end of it.'
His breath pong of
booze and
fags.
The screaming go on more –
Mămică start
when she come through the door.
'Do you believe this boy, Miri?' Tata say.
'Nicu, listen to Tata.'

His finger touch my head.
His breath touch my tummy.

'Nicu, Tata knows best,' Mămică say.
'But I want to stay here.' I praying to them.

'*Here*, what is here?' Tata say. 'People hate us *here*.'
'Nicu, people *here* only see our skin, not the thing
    within,' Mămică say,

thumping her bosom,
            two times.

We continue to
shout
scream
roar
yell
until I have no more voice.

# The Dregs

They say
we are the dregs
and
pack us off to the park to teach us a lesson,
where we
pick up crap
and
talk crap,
pay back
our society,
which we
*so*
wounded.

But take the rest of them – the other wrong'uns.

Rick's got a temper,
might batter you if you
talk dirt about his mum
or whatever.

And Fiona's a bit of a crackpot,
tattoos up her arm like a footballer.
She's only here
cos some slag tried to bottle her
outside a nightclub.

Lee was done for selling weed
to kids in his class
(but looks like he smokes most of it himself).

Bill nicked a BMW
and was caught joyriding down the A10
like Lewis bloody Hamilton.

And Jade tagged tonnes of tube trains,
too stupid to realise they had the whole thing on
    camera.

So,
yeah,
we're not exactly angels,
probably a bit yobby,

but the dregs?

Do me a favour.

# EYES OF JESS

Many day at reparation scheme
Jess try to helping with my
English.

She say to me lots of important informations:
*FAG BREAK*
*BUNK OFF*
*KEEP AN EYE OUT*
*COMPLETELY KNACKERED.*

Rick, who is like *top boy* offender,
tell me that passing womens are
*WELL FIT*
but
I hearing *WEALTHY,*
which make Rick
and others
hyena laugh and friend-slap my back,
though
Jess give me special eyes
when peoples are
*TAKING THE PISS.*

Rick
definitely taking my piss when
he ask me to shout
*CAN I WARM MY HANDS IN YOUR MUFF?*
to Dawn.

And when these *TAKING THE PISS* things
happen,
I always search for the special eyes of Jess.

Always
I
search.

# Pairing Up

I spend two hours
scrubbing graffiti from a kids' climbing frame,
then meet Nicu by the park gates.

We seem to be doing this a lot,
and I can't remember how it happened,
how we paired off from the others,
and I stopped smoking cheeky fags
with Fiona and Rick,
started sharing a bag of
Maltesers with Nicu instead.

'You want I walking you home?' he asks.
'I protect you from bears.'
He growls and flexes his muscles,
kisses both fists.

I laugh. 'Ain't no bears in Wood Green, mate,
and you know it.'

He laughs too. 'I protect you from
bad boy robbers instead,' he says.

'How about I walk *you* home
to protect *you* from bad boy robbers,' I say.

'Sounds like first class deal to me,' he says,
and tries to take my hand,
like,
actually hold my hand
as though we're going out together
or something.

I pull away.

I don't need anyone touching me.

'Unless you plan on walking out in
front of a car,
I don't think
we need to hold hands,
do you?' I ask.

He smirks. 'Worth trying, Jess,' he says.

'Yeah,' I say. 'It was worth a try.'

# MISTER INVISIBLE MAN

Woman are complicate.
One day
up,
one day
weirder.

At school I thinking that
maybe Jess has really
two peoples
inside her brain.

She don't return my smile.
She don't give me the Jess special eyes.

I am Mister Invisible Man.

But I not want to make for her
difficult time
in case
she has boyfriend in the lad crew.

Mostly I not want Jess to lose her
pride
dignity
honours
if she friendly chatting with me.

I can be her protect from this.

Still,
it not feeling lovely to be
Mister Invisible Man.

# All Smiles

After litter picking
we go to the cheapest caff on Wood Green
   High Road.
I get a Coke.
Nicu orders a mug of tea
and smiles.

He's got a nice smile, Nicu,
even though
his teeth are a bit
      crooked.
His face sort of
  scrunches up,
      his eyes shine.
And I watch him slurp at his tea
while he tells me all about his life
back home,
how he lived in a house with no proper floor,
just dirt and dust on the ground,
and he rode donkeys and horses,
cos they didn't have money for a car.
   'And no skateboardings,' he says,
and smiles again,
      all shiny.

The woman behind him gets up
and goes to the counter to pay,

but she leaves her bag right there
on the seat,
    wide open
like a bloody invitation.
    'The bag,' I whisper to Nicu.
    'Tea bag?' he whispers back.
He looks into his mug,
stirs it with the spoon.

I don't hang about.
I sit next to him,
pretend to put my arm around his shoulder,
then slip my hand into
the woman's
fake Gucci
and find her phone.
Job Done.

Nicu doesn't have a clue what I'm doing,
thinks I'm trying it on,
and leans into me.
    'Relax, mate,' I tell him,
and drop the phone into the pocket of his blazer.

The woman comes back,
        grabs her bag
and is gone.

And then we're off too,

up the High Road to the Italian,
where we order meatballs
and salad,
a pizza with extra olives.
And for dessert two slices of tiramisu.
Thank
you
very
much.
'I like these eats,' Nicu says.


The waiter gives us the bill.


I rummage and rummage around my
bag,
pretending to look for my wallet.
'I left it at school. It's at school.
Oh, crap.
Have *you* got any money?'


'No.'
Nicu looks like he might
cry.
I told him it was my treat.
'I tell to you this.
I *tell* to you I have no monies!'
He's almost shouting,
frantic,
while the waiter looks on.

'Give him your phone,' I say.
I manage a wink.
Nicu blinks.

'Give him your phone.
It's in your pocket, Nicu.'
I point.
Nicu reaches into his blazer
and finds the iPhone.

I snatch it
and wave it at the waiter.
'Can we leave this here and come back?
I'll bring you the money for the bill in an hour.
No.
Half an hour.
I promise.'

I do a drama on him.
Make my voice *EastEnders* shaky.

He nods
and
lets us leave,
lets us swagger out of that place
without paying a penny.

'You make me bad boy,' Nicu says
when we get to the park.

We're on the slide again,
at the top of it,
chewing on liquorice laces.

'*I* made you a bad boy?
Oh, come on, Nicu,
I think you were a bad boy well before you met
     me,' I say.

And he gives me that smile.

# NEW TEACHER

On top of slide
I think I should say to her *my* secret,
my special confidential.
But I am afraid
in case Jess not understanding,
in case Jess slide away
and
          never come back.

I can't tell to her
how one day
I dream to escape Tata and Mămică
because of person *they* want me to become.
And
how I have too much shock thought every day
in and out my head
of seeing future wife in white bling dress.

Jess is the danger girl.
She is the danger to big plan that
Mămică and Tata have for me.

But she is also the helper girl.
She say she is going to teach me to speak proper
if it bloody well kills her.
'This will be the most help,' I say.
She say,

'You can't speak like a twat, if we are going to be
    mates, Nicu.'
'I agreeing, Jess. I not wanting to be twat.'
She puts her hand in face and giggling.
All this tell me one thing:
Jess is kindness.


When I ask:
'Jess, what is *mate*?'
she tell me
a mate is someone you can chat with.
'You know, about anything, secrets and that.
Stuff you don't tell your parents.'
'Like dreams?'
'Yeah, I suppose.'
'Confidentials?'
She rub my hair
        and butterfly float in my belly.
'You do this to mate?' I say.
'Only if I like them,' she say.
Maybe if I kiss her I can say:
*And this too?*
But I'm OK that Jess is my mate
(my first English mate),


so I stop thinking about kiss.

# Bad Friday

He sits in the library
at lunch,
flicking through books with loads of pictures
in them.

I see him on Wednesday
when I go in there with Shawna to
copy her homework.
He looks up,
but before he can wave or call out my name,
I turn my back on him.

And then on Thursday
Liz wants to photocopy some form for her mum
and he's in there again,
different book,
      same lonely look.

I just peer through the window on Friday,
and of course he's there again,
turning the pages
of some big book,
his eyes really wide.
'What you staring at?' Meg asks,
spooking me from behind.
'You know him or something?' she asks,
spotting Nicu.

'No,' I say quickly.
'Why would I?'
She snorts.
'Yeah, it's not as if you speak Polish or anything?'

'Exactly,' I say,
and we laugh,
like friends,
so loudly that Nicu turns.

He sees us.

And so I stop.

I stop laughing.

# THE BUTT

Before I coming to school
in new country,
I not understand how hard
it will be.
Education is very important thing
here.
Very important thing
for to get jobs,
cash,
houses,
holidays,
cars,
shoes.

Back in village,
going to school not so important for us children.
Political persons don't
care if I go or not.
Parents
same.
But,
back in village,
no person does the laughing at me
behind my face.

Even in front of my face
it happening.

In class,
out class,
in corridor,
out corridor,
in yard,
out yard,
in canteen,
all place.
Snigger, snort, chuckle,
chuck paper,
pens,
pretend knives, guns, bombs,
weapons of massive destruct into my feelings.

But
they don't seeing
what I seeing.
They don't hearing
what I hearing.
They don't emotion
what I emotion.

I think maybe Jess is different.

I want to know an answer.

# The Three Bitches

Liz is all like,
'That pikey's staring again, Jess.
I reckon you're in there!'
She smirks and
and Shawna goes,
'Eww, man, I think he really fancies you.'
She sticks out her tongue,
blue from the gobstopper she's been sucking,
and waggles it.
Meg lets out a laugh and says,
    'Maybe he wants to show you a good time in his
    caravan.'
Everyone in the corridor can hear,
and she thinks
it's well funny,
like we haven't heard the gypsy joke
a hundred times today
already.

She reaches into her locker and
    pulls out
a book,
holds it up:
*Big Fat Gypsy Weddings.*

Where the hell did she get that?
'Really?' I ask.

'What?' Meg high-fives Shawna,
and they squeal
like ugly sick pigs,
like nasty little witches about to brew up
something poisonous.
'Gonna cut out some pictures and post them around
the place,' Meg says.
'Might give a few to Dan, so he can
put 'em up in the changing rooms.'

Liz is like, 'That's *hil-ar-ious*.'

And I could say,
*But is it?*
*Is it hilarious?*
*Cos I think it's boring.*
*I think you're boring.*
*All of you.*
*And anyway he doesn't live in a caravan.*
*He lives in a flat.*

But I don't say anything
cos I don't wanna be on the receiving end
of Meg's bile.

'I've got French,' I say instead,
and turn away.

Behind me I hear whispering.

Nothing else.

I keep walking.

# TOSSING AND TURNING

I sleep bad these nights.

The *tip-tap-tip*
in my head
still happen in new country
because too many times
I thinking of Jess.

I thinking what Mămică and Tata would say
if they knew Jess was so much
in
my
mind.

Inside and out,

she is beauty full.

# Shag/Marry/Dump

'Right,' Meg says.
'Mr Pitcher, Mr Morgan and Mr Betts.'

Shawna screams.
'That's just *nasty*.
Can you even imagine?'

Liz laughs.
'No. Cos I'm not imagining,
but you must be.
Rank!'

The bell for the end of break
rings
but
Meg drags on her fag
like she hasn't heard it.
Everyone else smoking behind the drama block
leaves for their lessons.
'You've *got* to decide.
Shag, marry or dump?
Go!'

Shawna shrugs.
'Shag Mr Pitcher, marry Mr Morgan, and dump,
definitely dump, Mr Betts.'

Meg turns to me.
'You're quiet,' she says,
like it's a crime.
'This one's just for Jess.
Right,
Dan, Kenny and . . .'
She pauses.

Shawna and Liz wait with their mouths open.

I see the horrible machine of Meg's mind
as she searches for the name.

His name.

I cross my fingers that it won't be him,
that she'll say Ryan,
cos he's the most obvious choice.

Then she finally says it:
'Nicu.
Go on then, Jess.
Shag, marry, dump?'

It's a trap.

I mean,
I know it's a trap,
so I say,

'I'm not getting married, Meg.'

'Why? You a lezzer?' she asks.

Shawna moves away from me,
            just a bit.
Liz chucks her fag.

'It's a crap game,' I say.
'We played it in Year Eight
and it was crap then,
too.'

Meg throws her fag butt on to the ground,
grinds it to dust with the heel
of her shoe.

'Do you fancy Dan or something?' she asks.
I almost
crack up laughing.
That's what she thinks?
That I fancy Dan?

'Know what, Meg,
you can shag them *all*.
But it's a good job it is a game
cos I don't think anyone'll
be queueing up to shag you.'

# THE LAST LAUGH

*Big Fat Gypsy Weddings* pictures
are in everywhere:
school changing place,
canteen,
locker,
and
teacher board.

Many photos of
wives with
epic dress and comic hair
or
husbands with
golden smiles and diamond eyes.

I don't rip pictures away.

I don't rip away
because
these gypsy weddings are
not my peoples,
not my weddings,

not my me.

So
I have last laughing.

After very short timing
*Big Fat Gypsy Weddings* pictures
look sad,
like death sunflower.

Finally,
they flop down
dead.

And
I have one more
last laughing.

# A Quick Word

I'm washing gunk off my hands
after pointlessly playing with
papier mâché for two hours,
when Dawn moseys over.
'Can I have a quick word, Jess?'

I show her my sticky palms and say,
'One sec,'
knowing her *quick word*
will totally turn into some
clock-watching psycho session.

'Just wondering how you're finding the scheme.
Any positives from this whole thing yet?' she asks.

'Uhh, like what?'

'I don't know. Have you learned anything?'

'Dunno.'

'Or maybe you made a friend?'

I sneer.
'Friends?
With that lot? Yeah, right.
You must be joking.'

Nicu is on the other side of the room.
He waves a papier mâché pig
and gives me a thumbs up.

I guess Nicu is my friend.
In a way.
We hang out,
I can rely on him and he's never tried
to hurt me.

So why haven't I given him
my number?

I mean,
what would be the harm?

# NUMBERS

On eat and fag
break at
reparation scheme,
the others message
on phones with
fast fingers.

Everyone do swapping of numbers.
Not me.
I go to pond and
swap sweets with swans.

I hear foot crunching on stone.
　'Hey, you didn't give me your number,' Jess say.
My breath become heavy weight.
'You want *my* number?' I say.
'Yeah, what is it?'
I tell it to her,
and
she tell hers to me.

And I photograph hers in my head.

# Quite Nice

I've no shortage of boys
wanting me,
after me,
telling me
I'm the golden sun
and bloody silver moon.

In Year Seven
    Keith Woods
passed me a note
in science
that said
'*Your reelly cute!*'
and I let him
kiss me with
his mouth open
more than once,
his tongue
far too flappy
for my liking.

In Year Eight,
    Michael Mensah
asked me out,
and I said *yes*,
and spent the next three weeks
battling with him

while he fought to
get my bra off.

In Year Nine
    Noah Stein
told everyone
I was hot,
and I liked that,
and when he put his
hand up my skirt
I didn't say no.
Not the first time anyway.

And this year,
    even though I'm still in Year Ten,
    a load of sixth formers have been
        chatting me up after school,
    messaging me,
    saying stuff that would make Mum's eyes
        water.

But it's all the same.

It's all about *them*.
What they want.
What *I* can give.

Down the youth offenders' place
    Nicu Gabor

talks to me
and listens to me
and wants to do things for me.

His voice dances
with words that are all messed up
but actually mean something,
and whenever we're together
he makes me
laugh
and laugh,
sometimes until my ribs hurt.

Nicu:
        he's more than quite nice.

# GIFTS AND TALENTS

How do English boys impressing the girls?
Chocolate?
Cider?
Car?
What is the secret?

I want to impressing Jess with being
her listener,
her joker,
her doer.

Maybe if she see me back in Pata
as talent wrestler,
making throws
and
takedowns,
she be in the full impress with me.

# Cleaning

I know I was young
cos I couldn't
work Terry's phone properly.
I took a ten second video of my own face
before he snatched it back.
'Are you stupid? This. Here. The red button.'

He hadn't beaten Mum up,
just given her a toothbrush and told her
to clean the toilet
while he watched.

But then he got bored,
wanted to see the end of some Spurs match,
so that's when he had the idea to give me his phone,
to record it,
save the memory of Mum on her knees.

'And next time the bathroom's a pigsty,
I'll make you clean it with your tongue,' he warned
    her.

Mum didn't answer.
She just nodded
and reached for the bleach.

'Record until she's done,' he told me. 'Got it?'

'Yeah,' I said,
and as he left the bathroom
Mum glanced up at me,
and I knew then that Terry had forced
me to be on his side,
    leaving Mum on the other,

            leaving Mum alone.

I knew right then
that Terry had found a
very important
role for me.

# HATE PAGES

On my mathematic book
some peoples write:
*Isis Slag.*

On my science book
some peoples write:
*Taliban Gooooooo Home.*

On my French book
some peoples write:
*Voted out of Britin Fuck Off.*

On my mathematic book again
some peoples write:
*Rat Boy Gypsy Scum.*

On
English
geography
history
book
they write:
*Stinking Gyppo.*

I do ripping of hate pages.

# Scribble

Nicu and I are only in one lesson together –
design technology,
and
while he's up at the teacher's desk
getting something checked,
Dan grabs his work book
and scrawls
*Stinking Gyppo*
across it.

'Dick!' I say aloud.

Meg sniggers into her hand.
'Yeah, you should tell Dan to write that on his
    maths book
next lesson.'

I don't bother telling her I'm actually talking about
    Dan.

'Dick,' I say again,
this time
looking right at Meg.

# BAD TACKLE

If you not do school homework
you do
detention
for to write
punishment words.

But

I don't write punishment words.
I look out window at P.E. teacher playing football
    with crew lads.

I see.

I see
crew lad football tackle into Obafemi.

I see
geezers laughing,
Obafemi foot holding.
Teacher doing the five highs with Dan and other
    crew.

I see
everything.

# Don't Make It Easy

Terry's got the paper open in front of him
on the kitchen table
and he's jabbing at some article
with his finger,
prodding a picture of
a slightly scruffy bloke
like he might actually be able to hurt
him a bit
by attacking the newspaper.
'They're only here five minutes
and the council's putting them in houses
down Lordship Lane.
It's disgusting.
Taxpayers' money
putting up scroungers
who'd pimp out their
own kids for a pound.'

I want to roll my eyes
and make Terry
tell me exactly where these foreigners
are living.
Because I've *seen* the estate where
Nicu lives and it's worse than
this one –
windows covered in
bed sheets,

gangs of kids everywhere
and loads of people with dogs on chains –
a total hellhole.
I say,
'Yeah, it's terrible, Terry.'

'Are you taking the mick?' he says.

'No,' I say
quickly.
'No, I mean it, it's terrible.
Loads of foreign kids at school too.'

'Well, I hope you don't make it easy for them,' he
        says.

I shake my head.
'Nah, I don't make it easy,' I say,
thinking of Nicu.

And actually,
this isn't even a lie.

# THE GHOST

At school I try to be so much low key,
to not catch her gazing
or
have my body in her space.

Sometime I follow like ghost
to where she goes:
I sit behind in canteen,
so I can watching her without notice,
spy her hair flowing,
her shoulders dancing when she laugh.

One time I see her white skin between
jumper
and
trouser.
A dream!
Like desert oasis.

And she never see my follow,
my spy,
my ghost.

But my voice, hair, skin
don't make easy my blending in.
Maybe
I need to do

gel style hair
like Dan and his crew,
show my undergarments
above tracksuit,
walk more like
gangster man.

Maybe then I can becoming
important
part of here.

Big
question mark.

# A Bit Much

Liz is all like, 'He keeps *staring* at you!'
And Shawna says,
'Doesn't he wash his hair?'

I take a bite from my limp pizza
and say, 'I'm doing time with him
      down the park.
He said he used to ride a pony or a horse or
   something back home.
He's funny.'

'You mean he actually *is* a pikey?' Meg says.
'I never said that.'
'Yeah . . . he's probably one of them Roma ones.'
'Maybe. So what?'
'So *what*? So *brilliant*.'

One side of Meg's mouth twists into a smile and
I know then
I should've kept schtum.
Information like that is jackpot gold
to a bitch like her.

'Oi, gypsy boy! Oi, gypsy boy!
When you gonna show us your donkey kong?'
Meg shouts across the canteen.

Nicu doesn't look up.
Just keeps chewing on a roll,
gazing out the window.
But Dan and his gobby mates have heard,
sidle over.
'What's happening?' Dan asks.

Meg cups her hand around Dan's ear
then puts her lips to it,
whispering,
whispering,
thinking she's so hot and mysterious.

And I know what comes next.

'*Ee-aw! Ee-aw!*'
It starts with Dan.
Not that loudly.
Then his mates join in.
'*Ee-aw! Ee-aw!*'
Then Meg too.
'*Ee-aw! Ee-aw!*'
Nicu still doesn't know that this crap is
aimed at him.
He's smiling at a dinner lady now,
with that puppy smile
that makes her *well* happy –
I mean, she's like forty years old.
Why wouldn't she love that face?

Dan picks up his plate
and marches over to Nicu.
He thinks he's Kanye bloody West.
Everyone knows Dan lives with both parents in a
    massive semi
up Crouch End way.
Thinks he's a rude boy.

I watch.
Can't look away.
Know I should leave.
Know I should tell someone.
Know I should do something.

But
come on,
this is Dan Bell-end we're talking about.
Standing up to him would be
one hundred per cent suicide.

Nicu looks up.
        At last.
But smiles
        too sweetly,
        too innocently,
        too much like a typical foreigner
        who just doesn't get it.

Until he does.

Until Dan tips his chips over Nicu's head.
Until they are tumbling down his shoulders.
Until ketchup is slathered through his hair and
Dan is laughing,
and his mates are laughing,
and most of the idiots in the room are laughing.
Then
Meg saunters over and casually launches half a
     muffin
at Nicu's face.

'A bit much,' I murmur.

And Liz is like, 'So what? He's *weird*.'
And Shawna says, 'I think the hair's an improvement
actually.'

Nicu is silent.

His hand curls around his carton of apple juice.
The sparkle trickles out of him,
and I'd bet anything
that in his head he's telling himself to be
*a good boy, a good boy.*

I mean,
what else can he do
with Dan and his boys surrounding him,
hoping it'll kick off?

I can't stay.
Can't see any more.

'Fuck this,' I say
and, leaving my tray where it is,
go for a smoke behind the drama block.

# RED FACE

I see on floor
chips and
red
ketchup.
Happy is not my blood.

My only happiness.

I see the angry in Jess face,
angry not at me,
at them.

I see her push door with
aggressive and leave.

Leave everyone in the laughter
at my pain.

# Picking

I blow smoke rings into the air.

Without turning around I know
Nicu's there,
ketchup in his hair,
and he's looking at me.

I pretend not to sense him,
concentrate on my fag.

I pick
at a thick, hard scab on my hand.

I just know he's not
   looking away
or curling up his nose
or going to say, 'Don't pick, Jess, so ranking,'
or do anything else to
make me feel
disgusting
– which I am
   sometimes.

Not to him
though.

Not ever.

And
I don't know why
but
it doesn't feel good.

I keep waiting for him to see through me
or just see me
as I am,
and when he does
he'll be pretty
disappointed.

# HATING THINGS

I hate
morning interval,
lunchtime eating,
afternoon break,
people looking and jokes they make.

I hate
P.E. lesson because I can't kick ball
like lads here.
Crazy teacher howls, *'Nicu, Nicu, Nicu!'*
Some do fouls on my legs
with purpose.

I hate
P.E. showers because
I don't want
them
seeing
my naked.

I hate
Dan and crew doing cock helicopters
near to my face,
slapping my arse with towel.
I can't to scream
cry
freak

run out of the place.
That would
tell crew
I'm the easy prey.

I hate
the day someone put note
on no-hope table:
*Brexit!!!*

I hate
being target board for
their every
dart.

# As If Nothing Happened

Standing around waiting
for Nicu at the youth centre
my mind is going mental:
I'm so over
these team-building activities,
I'm so bored with
Dawn's sessions
and
I've had it with
all this reparation bullshit.

Nicu bounces out of
Bicep Andy's office,
which makes me feel
even worse.

'Hi, Jess,' he says,
as if nothing ever happened
in the canteen the other day,
like he's forgotten all about it.

'Nicu, I'm sorry. I was well out of order,' I say
    quickly.
'Sorry? For why?'
'For what happened in the canteen.'
'You do no bad to me, Jess.'
'Shut up. You know I should've said something.'

'Jess, if you walk with wolf, it not mean you *are* wolf.'

He nods.

I don't really get what he means.

Doesn't matter though.

I already feel a bit better.

'Thanks, Nicu.'

'No thanking me. You are not my evil, Jess.'

# ACTIVITY CIRCLE

Boy team activity circle
have also Dawn and Bicep Andy
as our lead.

We do many talkings about
home,
school,
futures,
fears.

Rick say he want to be footballer.
Lee say he want to be millionaire.
Bill say he want to marry model.

'What about you, bruv?' Lee ask.
'Yeah, Nicu, what you want to do, mate?' Rick
    ask.
All heads eyeing me.
I say:
    'I never want go to man prison.'

All boy team big time laugh.
Me too.
'I hear that, Nicu,' Bill say. 'I hear that.'

When Dawn and Bicep Andy
leave circle,

Rick come to me.
Standing over.
'Oi, Nicu.'
'Rick.'
'Question.'
'OK.'
'How do you say *fuck this shit* in your language,
    mate?'

When I telling Rick answer
all boy team big time laugh
again.

Me include.

# My Future

Now we're studying for proper exams,
it's not just Mr Morgan
banging on about us fulfilling our potentials.
Every teacher is like,
'It's about time you lot took school seriously,'
and
'If you applied yourself, you could
*blah blah blah,*'
and
'What do you want to do after your exams anyway?
Have you thought about college?'

I could say,
'Well,
I wanna be a doctor
with my own practice down
Harley Street
and make four hundred quid an hour.
But
if that isn't possible
maybe I could
work in films,
and make stuff
that everyone watches.
Or
if,
you know,

like,
I don't get great results,
I could do an apprenticeship or something
like my aunt Helen
who works as a hairdresser on a cruise ship.'

But
the thing is,
it doesn't matter what I want,
how smart I am
or what results I get –

    people like me
    never get out
    of places
    like this.

# HANDS

When I exit Bicep Andy office,
Jess is there again,
sitting in plastic chair.
She wait for to meet Dawn.

My body goes wobbly.
'All right?' she say.
'I all right,' I say.
'Crap this, innit?' Jess say.
'Suck job,' I say.
Jess does laughing.
'Suckest job ever,' I say.
'Exactly.'
'You want chocolate button?' I ask.
'I'll have two,' Jess say.

Jess looking gloom.
        I sit down.
'What is matter?' I ask.
'Nothing,' she say.
'Tell to me.' I friendly punch her.
'Just leave it, Nicu.'

I want to find her world,
to see what she see,
to pain with her pain.

Most of all
I want my hand to touching hers,
but I just
        leave it.

# Why Won't He?

I can't persuade him
to even take one drag
of my fag
and
it sort of pisses me off sometimes
that he won't do it,

that he won't keep me company.

'You're such a baby,' I say,
which is a bit weak,
but it's cos I don't really know
how to insult someone
who has his
own mind.

# THE WRESTLER

After park workings
my bones are exhaust,
my back is shatter
and
my stomach sing for Mămică's soup stew.

I thank all gods we have
only one week to finishing.

This work make me never stealing from any shop
ever.

When I coming in my home
I don't smell Mămică's soup stew,
or
hear clatter of cooking.
My belly rolls with groans.

Out of the nowhere,
laughing hit my ears.

Mămică and Tata.

Mămică and Tata
in living room.

Alone.
        Laughing.
        Alone.
            Noising.

        Sexing?

I freeze to my spot,
and I wanting so much that black hole
swallow me up.
            No. No. No. No. No. No. No.

'Nicu!' Tata shout.

I schtum it.

'Nicu!' Mămică shout.

My breath schtum.

'Nicu, come here,' Tata shout again.
'We want to show you something.'

My heart almost schtums too.

'Nicu, get your arse in here,' Tata say in louder
    voice
because he think
I am far.

On my enter all is
OK.

I see them looking at
Tata's phone,
bodies together, eyes watching, faces sunny.

'Look, Nicu,' Mămică say, 'look what we found on
    Tata's phone.'
'It's from last year,' Tata say.
'You look much younger,' Mămică say.
'But strong as a bison,' Tata say.

Over shoulders
I look also the phone and see it.
See me.

Body low.
        Head up.
Feet wide.
Ready to do classic takedown move.

'You could have been a proper champion,' Tata say.
'A national champion,' Mămică say.
'An Olympic champion,' Tata say. 'First famous
    Gabor ever.'

And I was dreaming this too
long times ago.

Gold,
silver
or
bronze.
Any of three.

But dreams flutter high in air.
     *Bye-bye*
wrestling butterfly.

Hello
husband.

# Looking for an Excuse

I won't miss Dawn, or Bicep Andy
or any of the navel-gazing crap
they make us do here.

But I hate it ending

cos,
like,
how am I gonna find an excuse to be
with Nicu?

# PARTY

Fiona
Bill
Rick
Jade
Jess
Lee
me
   everyone say *see you laters* in shed.

So much noise,
laughing,
piss-take,
smoking.
I not understanding chat banter
but I understanding
the happy face on guys
for
final day of youth offender work.

In shed party
Fiona and Jade sink cider,
Bill and Rick spark roll-up,
Lee pump tunes from iPhone.

Me and Jess
share good time
conversation.

# When Terry Is Out

I find one of
Terry's old phones hidden
        at the back of his wardrobe
and watch
through films I helped make.

Pan shot of the living room:
TV, sofa and sideboard.
A normal enough flat until
there's the
zoom shot of Mum screaming –
then
cut to
Terry laughing and kicking,
        his fists flying
        and
        my
        voiceover saying quietly,
        'Please stop, Terry.
        Please stop.'

Finally it
fades out.

        He's telling Mum
what set him off,
and she's saying sorry

again

    and again
    and again.

My finger hovers over the delete button,
but I don't do it.

    I can't.

I put the camera back in its hiding place
and
go out to look for Nicu,
who isn't anywhere.

He can't always be there

and I shouldn't
expect him to be.

# PHOTOGRAPHS

There is
**X**
in calendar
in big, thick pen.

When we have
wedding day
celebration.

On coffee table
they spreading photo of marriage girls
night
after
night.

I will need
all my skills for
wrestling out of damn situation.

See,
they want me to tell who I pick.

I can't to tell.

And
I can't to tell Jess.

# Falling

It's the first free Saturday for three months.
And I don't have to,
but I spend it with Nicu
on a patch of grass
behind his flats.

He won't stop messing around,
making faces,
telling jokes,
and then he
unlaces his right trainer,
does the same with my left.

I don't shoo him away
or smack the back of his hand.
I watch
as he ties our laces together,
binds us.

'Up! Come with me,' he says,
and tries to stand,
but of course he can't
cos
I stay sitting like a stone
with my eyebrows raised,
being as cool as I can.
'Bit old for three-legged races,
aren't we?'

'Come. I want to try,' he says,
so I stand,
finally,
our legs pressed up against each other.

He throws one arm around my shoulder.
'For to balancing,' he says.

I put my arm around his shoulder too.

And we shuffle,
his left foot forward
        my right foot forward,
then
my left and his right together.

We walk slowly,
        awkwardly,
        laughing and on the
verge of falling.

We don't get far.

But we do manage to move.

        We do get
        somewhere
        tied together like that.

# DOUBLE OH SEVEN

On Internet I see the old film of James Bond.
This spy man have all he want:
the girls,
the fashions,
the cars.

I practise my James Bond,
chatting up ladies
in front of mirror.
   *Hi there, girl, would you care to share cocktail drink?*
   *Do you like to be in my car?*
   *Can I unzipping your garment?*

Then I change,
I am special agent
Nicu Gabor
and I imagine asking to Jess:
   *Do you like to be in my pleasure?*
   *Can you show me to your world?*
      *Would you enjoy dating day with me?*

This final question is what I will ask to Jess.

# No Answer

My phone
pings.

> **Wanna go 4 a Macky Ds l8r**
> **wiv me, Shawna + Liz?**
> **Meg xxxxxx**

A few months ago
I would've said
*YES.*

Now I don't even bother answering.

I text Nicu.

# ICE NATION

When Mămică and Tata tell to me about
all the peoples who will be gifting me
presents for wedding,
I have great fear.
I think that one day
I will returning from school to become
Victim of Kidnap Plot.
Hood on head.
Gag in mouth,
taken away to old place for to be
meeting and married to
stranger.

I know that this will happen.
I know I have not the power to stop.
But.
I need Jess.
I must to make her my
only and one.
It is essential for offer myself to her.
First to be date partner.
Second to take my heart:
       for Jess to be my kidnapping.

# Sometimes

I wanna say to Nicu,
'I'm way out of your league,'
or
'Look at me, and look at you,'
but I don't.

And I'm not sure why.

# GOOD FUN TIMES

The day I ask to Jess is like
World War III
in my chest.
I am too much shitting my bricks.

'Tell me you're having a laugh, Nicu?' Jess say.
'I not laughing, Jess. I dead serious.'
'What, like a *real date*?' she say.
'It will be nicest of days,' I say.
'With *me*?' Jess say, looking with her demanding
    eyes.
'We will have good fun times.'
'Suppose so.'
'Proper dating. In night-time,' I say.
I swear Jess eyes
fill with the
tears.
She kick stones,
small,
big,
bigger,
away into the distance.

'And I like your gorgeous physical,' I say,
because all the girls need knowing this.
'That's sweet.'

'So we go on night date then?' I say.
'We can go out at night,' she say. 'But it is *not*
    a date.'

*WE CAN GO OUT!*

I want to
jump,
cheer,
whoop.
Sit on nine clouds.

Jess
say
YES.

'I thinking Burger King
or
greasy spoon,' I say,
because these are
English date places.
    'No,' Jess say. 'Let's do something better.'

I swallow grenade.

Does Jess meaning that we do . . .?
That we should to . . .?
That we . . .?

'Let's go up Ally Pally,' she say.
'Ally Pally?'
'Alexandra Palace.
They've got a massive ice rink there.
Can you skate?'
'Yes.'

I tell white
little lie.

# Effort

I don't wear much make-up usually,
can't be bothered with bright lipstick or thick
   eyeliner
that all the other girls go for.

I never normally wear perfume.

But I do today
because I'm going out with Nicu.

And I don't want him to
think
I didn't make an effort.

# ONE BOY FALLING

On bus to Ally Pally
I can smelling my Tata's
man-splash
that I tap on
cheek and chin.
My date clothes have condition washing,
and my
special occasion leather jacket
make me handsome man.

Jess smell of
summer day in lovely garden.
She have skinny jeans,
red lips,
black lines under eyes,
hair like the girl band.
Bus people stare
because she is complete
wow vision.

We don't do much speaking on bus.
We staring at world outside.

The skating is not graceful romance like Olympics.

Music DJ plays
*doof*
       *doof*
              *doof!*
Lights flash
red,
green,
blue.
   'Hey, guys, welcome to Ice Nation!' DJ shout.

Boys, girls, dates, friends, gangs
ferocious fly in their skates,
zip zoom.
Ice spraying every place.

I hold on to side.

'I thought you could skate?'
Jess saying with snigger.
'It is different ice in Romania.'

I fall
five,
ten,
double ten
times.
My clean clothes and leather

get
wet.

Jess does *whoosh* circle alone
and backways skate too.
She could be professional ice woman.

I leave holding side
and bang my bum arse.
   'Come on,' she say with hands out to me.
I reach for her.
She slide closer.

We touch
fingers.
         Fingers become chain link.

They snake.

We touch
hands.

No . . .
We *hold* hands.

And the electric
flows
between our skin,

bones,
bodies.

We make three big circle around rink
with hands holding –
always holding –
and it's the most
magic amazing minutes of
my life.

I want so many more.

And
more.

# Same as You

A few days after Ally Pally,
after skating around the rink like
happy
kids at Christmas,
Nicu and I meet near the Tube station
and I tell him exactly what to do.

'You watch them coming through
the barrier,
and if they put a ticket in
and it
       pops out
again,
it's probably a Travelcard,
and *that's* what we want.
You understand what I'm saying?'

He nods. 'I understand, Jess.'

'Good.
Then, just as they get out of
the station,
you ask if they've finished with the card
cos you have to get to Holloway
to see your sick dad or whatever.
You get me?'

He nods again. 'I get you, Jess.'

'Then you give the cards to me,
and I'll sell 'em on to
the people at the ticket machines
for half of what they'd usually pay.
Right?'

He gives two thumbs up. 'Right, Jess.'

And then we get going,
blagging tickets,
selling them on,
making a fiver a time
until I've got fifty quid
in the back pocket of my jeans
and Nicu has two spare
Travelcards to get us into London.

So we take the Tube,
the Piccadilly Line all the way to
    Leicester Square,
and from there straight into
Häagen-Dazs, where I order the fattest cone
they've got and four scoops of
cookie dough ice cream.
'What do you want?' I ask Nicu.

'I want same as you, Jess,' he says,
eyes so fixed on my face that
I blush.
'All time same as you.'

# RHINO HANDS

Metal collecting give Tata dirt and oil hands,
like rhino skin.

I can't to keep eyes off those rhino hands.
Mămică stand behind
with palms in pray position.
It like
Heaven and Hell
are standing in living room.

Tata have two photo picture,
one for each dirt hand.

I scare to look.

Mămică and Tata have sunbeam on their faces.

'We've found her, Nicu,' Mămică say.
'Well, we're down to the last two,' Tata say. 'Two
    lovely girls.'
    He holding these *two lovely girls* up to my eyes.
'Have a look, Nicu, and tell us who's your
    favourite,' Mămică say.
'I've spoken to both families. They're happy with
    what I've offered them.'
'So it's down to you now, son.'

Right rhino thrust:
  'She's called Ana-Maria.'

Left rhino thrust:
    'She's called Florica.'

I look
at both photos
with concentrate.

But I seeing only
Jess.

# Liam

Nicu flicks my ear and I scream out,
try to give him a dead leg
and we bust our arses laughing
until a shadow appears over us.

'Jess?'
It's Liam.
He's got a bit of a goatee,
brown with flecks of ginger,
but he looks good.
As usual.
　'You all right?' he says.

I feel Nicu watching,
wondering who this bloke is,
this mad-good-looking bloke
who can get any girl he wants.

'I heard you got nicked,' Liam says.
'It was ages ago, Liam.'
'Yeah.'
He pulls out a packet of fags and offers me one.
I take it
and we walk away,
Nicu's eyes burning into my back.
I feel them,
and I wish he wouldn't do it –

look at me like that all the time –
like I'm
Someone.


'Where the hell have you been?' I ask Liam.
'It's been over a year for fuck's sake.
You didn't even tell me you were going
and now
it's a nightmare at home.
You have to come back.'


Liam shakes his head,
flicks ash at some flowers.
'Terry still around?'


I nod.


'Still knocking Mum about?'


I nod again.
　'Way worse than ever.
You've gotta come home, Liam.
He'll kill her
if you don't come back.'


Liam looks up at the sun.
Right into it.
　'I got my own problems, Jess.
Leila's pregnant.'

Leila,
the girl on the estate
who did drug runs for everyone?
That Leila?

'I'm living with her over in Tottenham now.
You could visit,
if you want.
Sometime.
That's what I wanted to say.
I wanna see you more.
I mean,
I wanna see you again.
I feel like a total dick for leaving,
but I couldn't stay.
Someone would have ended up dead.'

'OK.'

'Council gave us a flat.'

I look up at the sky myself
but the sun's gone –
heavy clouds hang low overhead.

He roots around in his pocket and pulls out a
    tenner,
stuffs it into my hand.
    'I'll see you around, yeah.

I'll call you,' he says.
But I know he won't call.

'Who was heart throb?' Nicu asks
when I walk back.

'Mind your business, Nicu,' I say,
and punch him in the arm,
when what I really want
is for him
to give me a hug.

# THE CHANGING PLACE

Teacher of P.E.
blows whistle,
scream my way,
   'Come on, son, toughen up!'
I rubbing my knee because some idiot dick
kick it hard on the purpose.

P.E. teacher does fast walking to my direction,
swinging arms,
steam in ears.
My knee blinks with pain.
'What is it?' he say when closer.
   'My knee hurting,' I say.
'What?'
   'My knee.' I try to tell to his ears and eyes.
But P.E. teacher don't care of my agony.
'If you knew the difference between a ball and a
   kebab then maybe you wouldn't get yourself
   hurt,' he say.
   'Yes, sir.'
Asad and Bilal look at grass.
Dan and mates do evil stare.

'Get up off your arse,' teacher say.

Red come to my face.
Fists get tight.

No reply.
Instead
I fast run to changing room.

P.E. teacher screaming more until I hear fading in
   his voice,
like I run inside cave.

After what happen in changing room
I don't do more football lessons.

After what happen in changing room
I don't want to go to school.

After what happen in changing room
big part in my heart
think Tata could be right when he say:
   'People here will never accept us.
They treat us like animals.'

But other part in my heart
think not all people see us like that.

Jess, for number one,
because she tell to me,
'The way I see it, if you're a dick, you're a dick,
so it doesn't matter what country you come
   from.'

But Dan definitely disagreeing with Jess
because
in changing room
he call me,
'a filthy, fucking thief,'
as he can't to find
his pen.
His pen with words *Chelsea Football Club* on it.

One mate with neck muscle say,
   'I bet he nicked it,
when he pissed off from football earlier, Dan.'

Two mate with the punk rock hair say,
'They'd rob from the
blind given half the chance.'
But I not know what he mean.

Three mate with fat belly say,
'Yeah, my old man's right about them lot.'
But I never one time meet his old man.

Dan and crew make the circle around me.
I try to put my sock on
but Punk Rock Hair
yank it
from my toe
and try to

throw on top of locker.
        It miss
        and hit wet floor.


Neck Muscle say,
    'You should do him, Dan.'
Punk Rock Hair say,
    'Break his nose.'
Fat Belly say,
    'Or his fingers.'
Then all I hear is
*RA*
*RA*
*RA*
because every boy shout in
my face,
so very close that I feeling their
mouth spit as it hit my
cheek
chin
eye
ear.


Then another great
yank come.
Massive yank on my hair.
Dan's hand is
strong and mighty.

My head is pull back,
my eyes see roof,
my heart like music:
*Boom!*
*Boom!*
*Boom!*
Dan come close like maybe he want to
kiss.
'If I find out you robbed my Chelsea pen,
you stinking gyppo twat,
I'm going to slice you
from here
to here.'
He do finger line across face
from ear
past cheek and mouth
to destination other ear.
'Got it?' he say.
'Got it,' I say soft.
But I don't
*got it*,
his stupid football pen.

'Right, come on, lads,' Dan say.

Before leaving changing room
Fat Belly kick my knee.

The sore shoots
between my legs,
but I stay silence.


Neck Muscle sniff up until his face become red,
his mouth full.
He spit
on side of my head.
But I again silence.


Punk Rock Hair do nothing,
laughs only.
Still I silence
while
my blood boiling with angry
and violence.


After they going
I pick up my
sogging sock.
The toe part is dry
so I use for towel
my eye sockets
and
clean Neck Muscle spit
from my head.


As I leaning to pick up bag
I spy it.

Like long plastic cigarette
lying dead under bench.
I roll it over with my
toe,
all the way
until *Chelsea Football Club* shine
up at me.

# On the Grass

Ally Pally again.
But not to skate,
just to sit up there
and watch London
spread out below us like an untouchable 3D map.
'Weird, isn't it?' I say.

Nicu is next to me on the grass
pulling apart dead leaves.
'What so weird?' he asks.

'I dunno.
Just that there are millions of
people in London,
and everyone thinking they're so important.
But if,
like,
a giant came along
and
squashed them,
hardly anyone would care.
Everything would go on as normal.'

'News reporting would care,' Nicu says.
He cups his hands over his mouth,
making his voice dramatic.
'Killer giant squash all citizens in London.'

I laugh.
'Yeah, but you get what I mean?'

He is silent. Maybe he doesn't understand.
Sometimes it's like that,
and not just cos of the language.

He rests a hand on my knee.
'You meaning *we* not important, Jess.

   You wrong.

      We both *very* important
      enough.'

# THREE SEATS

Tata is not computer man.

I showing him much times
how to delete
his
Internet History Browse.

Tata is not strong student.

When I get computer
time,
it not the
sexy site
Tata looking at
that
shivers up my skin.

Skin shivers begin
when I see
the buying of
three seats
to Cluj-Napoca.

Three seats to take us away
from
here.

Three seats in three weeks.

To take me away from
Jess.

# Accused

I see it happen.

I mean I'm standing right there.

And what happens is
nothing.

One hundred per cent
zero.

Meg is taking her books out of her locker,
moaning about some physics test,
when Nicu walks by,
brushes her with his bag,
and she turns
like a wild cat,
like a witch,
and pushes him against the opposite wall.

'Did you just touch my arse?' she shouts
in his face
and loud enough for the whole
corridor to hear her.

'What's going on?' my form teacher,
Ms Allen, wants to know,
coming out of her classroom.

'He touched me, Miss,' Meg says,
and starts to cry,
like,
proper tears.

'I not touched her,' Nicu says.
He holds up his hands
as if the truth were written
on to his palms.

'No, he didn't,' I say.
I stand forward.
I stand up
for Nicu for the first time.

'*Yes*, he *did*,' Meg says,
and gives me a glare.
A warning.
I look away so she enlists Shawna and Liz.
'Didn't he?
*You* saw him.'

They nod,
and if Ms Allen
wasn't standing right there
I'd claw them both.

'Right, everyone, come with me,' Ms Allen says.
Her face is flushed,

with pleasure, I think;
        she likes a good crisis.

'But Nicu didn't do it,' I repeat.
And
as though
Meg's conjured him up using black magic,
Dan appears.

Great.

'What's happening?' he asks.

'Him. He touched my arse,' Meg says.
Tears again.
Sobs.
Choking sounds
I've never heard from her before,
not even when her nan died
last year.

'Yeah, a thief and a perv,' Dan says.
'A little dickie bird told me he was on some
youth offenders' thing.'
He turns to Nicu.
'Rape you were done for,
weren't it, mate?'

Students slow down in the corridor –
stare and smirk
like it's some show at the O2.

Ms Allen's way out of her depth now.

'He. Didn't. Touch. Meg,' I say.

Dan puts his mouth to my ear as Ms Allen
tries to calm Meg down.
'That don't matter, Jess,' he whispers.
'What matters is that everyone *thinks* he did.'

# INNOCENT

It is filth lie what they say to me,
filth lie.
I do no arse touch
or
what Dan accuse.

I can't to prove
because I have no words for
defend myself.

So
I stand like stupid man in the train lights,
listening to Jess
doing
my defending.

Then I can't be stupid man no more.

I bolt away from all voices,
down long corridor,
past canteen
and find
my comfort.

In library.

# The Right Thing

Meg says, 'Oh my *God*,
did you see his face, though?
Classic.'
And they all crack up laughing
like an army of idiots.

I know there's nothing
I can do
to make them
more human,
but at least,
for once,
I didn't stand and watch
like someone had his hands around
my throat,
stopping me from speaking
          out.

For the first time in my life
I did the
right thing.

# VERY KIND

In library peoples are always giving Ms Nimmo the
    headache
because they don't stay in silence
or
they are giggling to their phones.
But Ms Nimmo doesn't do crazy off her nut at
    them.
Always she remain cool calm.
She smile,
throws eyes to sky,
tuts lips,
but never crazy nuts.

One day Ms Nimmo asked me about good things
    of Cluj,
the big city near Pata.
She sit with face near me.
I tell to her lots about my city:
our dramatic sun,
our photo panoramic,
our church cathedral.
    'Wow, I must go one day. It sounds beautiful,
    Nicu,' she say.
And she grinning.

On other day
she ask me to help lift

heavy box into office.

    'You're very kind, Nicu,' she say. 'Very kind
    indeed.'

And I grinning.


Today she say, 'You don't seem yourself, Nicu.

Everything OK?'

And even though I hearing only lies and jangle
  voices

inside my head,

I seeing too

Jess being my defence.

And I grin

the most

than ever before.

# Where Nicu Lives

'You sure they won't get
back early?' I say,
as Nicu turns the key
in his front door
and we step straight into his living room.
A kitchen runs along one of the walls.

'Don't worry, Jess.
Dad working
and Mum shopping to find bargains.'

The flat smells clean.
All the furniture is brown.

'I just don't want them going
nuts if
they find us
here,' I say.

'They go nuts only if
they finding us
doing sex,'
he says.

'Idiot,' I say,
but can't help snorting
into my hand,

trying to muffle the sound
like there could be someone else
at home.

I follow Nicu across the room
where he
opens the fridge and hands me a cold Coke.
I peer inside,
clock a big Tupperware box
filled with what look like sausage rolls.
'What are they?' I ask.

He takes out the box and opens it.
'Mum make herself.
Better than buying.'

'Yeah, but what are they?'

'It called sarmale. You never hear?'

'Never.'

'Very tasty.
I make one for you.'
He grabs a mushroom-coloured bowl from the
    countertop
and carefully
puts two rolls into it.

I wander away,
sit on the sofa,
stare at the coffee table
and the gleaming glass ashtray in the centre of it.

'Your parents smoke?' I ask.

Nicu looks over at me,
his eyes soft,
his lips pressed together.
'Dad smoking always.
It make Mum
*so* annoying.'

I laugh,
consider taking out my own fags
and lighting up,
but I don't
cos I know Nicu
wouldn't like it.

The only other thing on the coffee table is a photo
of a girl
in a flowery headscarf,
two plaits woven with coloured ribbons
at the front of her face.
She's pretty,
maybe our age,
maybe a bit older,

but she's staring into the lens
like it's a mugshot.

'This your sister?' I ask,
and wave the photo at him.

Nicu comes towards me holding the bowl.
He stops and stares.
'No,' he says,
'she not my sister.'

He puts down the bowl,
looks at his feet.

'Shit, she isn't your dead girlfriend or anything, is
    she?'
I ask.

But he's not laughing.
He looks at me again.
'Is not my fault,' he says.
'I not choose her.'

'What you on about, Nicu?'

'They choose wife for me,' he says.

'What? Who did?'

'Parents.
This girl in photo is name Florica.
She is the choose.'


'Wait a minute, so you're telling me that she's . . .'


'Florica is the wife choose.'


'Sorry, what? Your *wife*?'


'No, no. She is becoming wife after wedding.'


The rolls are steaming in the bowl.
I'm starving but
I suddenly don't like the look of them.


'My wedding.
They want us to getting married in nineteen days.'

# SAD WAVES

After I telling to Jess
story of Florica,
story of my cultures,
the gloom wave is over us.

I know she takes it hard to understanding
our ways,
our young age weddings,
our sarmale.

I finding it seriously hard too.

Life in England
make it all harder.

Jess make it the hardest.

# Nineteen Days

Who cares he's getting married?
It's not like *I* wanted to marry him.
It's not like I even fancy him.
He's a friend.
He can do whatever he likes.

But what sort of parents make their
kid marry someone they don't even know?

I keep thinking he's just like me,
that we get each other,
but I don't get this.

What is this?

It's bullshit, is what it is.

Nineteen days?

He can't though.

He just can't.

# DREAMLAND

And I dreaming of you last night,
but my eyes don't close for sleeping,
and it raining in my stomach,
and it storming in my heart.

And I thinking.
Thinking.

Thinking
of
us
together
for ever
and ever.

We never get lost
and
when I wake
I fear that our love will never be
found.

# Unheard

Shadows moving behind the front door.
A leg,
a head,
and I hear it too,
a thud,
a scream
and when I go in
Mum's lying in the hallway,
blood seeping into the rug,
Terry standing over her,
his phone on the hall table.

I'm afraid to help Mum.
But I can't just stand here and do nothing.
I can't be his accomplice any more.

'I'll call the police
if you touch her again,' I say.
My voice wobbles.
I know she's in for it now,
and that my big mouth has caused it.

But I'm wrong.

Terry sniggers,
looks like he's been expecting me to say
something like this,

and in one sharp movement
his hand is around my neck,
pressing me up against the wall.

'You speak to me like that again
and I'll give you something
to go to the police about.
You hear me . . . sweetheart?'
he hisses.

I can't breathe.
He holds me there,
squeezes.
'Now *fuck* off!' he shouts,
and pushes me away.

I walk backwards to my room.
'Mum,' I croak.

I don't think she hears me.

# SWISS ARMY

At the swan pond
we have throwing bread competition.
I throw most far,
my swan swim
fastest.
I am winner.

'All right, Nicu, calm down,' Jess say.
'I win prize?' I say.
Jess dig deep into her bag.
'Here,' she say, holding big green apple.
   'Not exactly a gold medal, but it *is* a Golden
   Delicious.'
'We share it,' I say.
Jess toss apple high. 'It's all yours.'
I catch one-hand. 'No, we share.'
'It's all right, really.'
'I insisting,' I say.

I do my own deep dig,
take out my
Swiss Army,
flick open
knife section.

'Jesus, Nicu,' Jess say.
'What? Swiss Army for surviving in wilderness

not for being town hooligan.'
'Right.'
I chuck Jess piece.
She catch one-hand.

When apple hitting our mouths
we look each other,
we nod each other,
we agreeing.

It true golden moment.

But gold moment like these
always
have black shadow in ceiling,
always
have thick fog in feeling,
always
have wedding and **X** day in my head.

And I can't to enjoying our
apple time.

# Transformation

I find a long piece of orange ribbon
Mum used to wrap the present she bought me
for my last birthday,
and cut the length of it
    in two.

Then I thread the pieces through my hair
and into long plaits
which lie against my face.

I take a towel from the radiator
in the bathroom
and wrap the back of my head in it,
try turning myself into the girl from the photo,
Florica – his wife in two weeks –
but I'm too pale to pass for her.

I'm studying my creation in my phone
when Mum comes into the room
looking for her hairdryer.

She blinks.
'Oh, you look nice,' she says.

I yank the towel off my head,
chuck it on the floor.
'I look ridiculous.'

'No. You look different.
Colourful.
You look pretty, Jess.'

She has sad eyes:
even when she's trying to be cheerful
she's a picture of misery.

I untie the plaits,
pull out the ribbons.
'Shut up, Mum.
I look like a dog
and we both know it.'

# BEWARE THE SILENCE

I curse myself
because it best to take
the end urinal for to
pee.

Not
middle one.

Stupid!

Here Dan and crew
can make easy
human sandwich
of me.

Here I can't escape them
because I peeing
streams and rivers.

Dan and henchman
say no swear,
do no shoulder pushing.

They let me pee.

I listening to splash from urinal,
sound of water fall

and
echo of our three
sounds.

I hearing crew breathings,
their whisper and laughing.
Like all is normal,
all is fine.

No speaking assaults.
No threaten.
No wicked eye.

It is worser.

It hitting my knee,
thigh,
shin.

Dan shake dry and exit with henchman.

When I hearing his giggle outside door
my body entire tremble.

# I Used to Walk to School with Meg

Not now.

I message Meg most mornings to say
I'm gonna be late,
I'm still in bed,
I'm not well,
so that she walks on without me,
and I prefer it.
I way prefer not having to make
small talk
with
someone
I wouldn't touch
to scratch.

# PING

My phone pinging,
Jess messaging
all times.

# Question

**Wanna go cinema?**

J x

# TOUCHING

We go to cinema to see
funny movie
romcom.
Jess show me how to sneaking past
without ticket buying.

In movie we drinking
massive Fanta.
We sharing
bucket popcorn.

In movie we touching
elbows together:
gentleness,
delightness.

And it feel like
voltage
speeding through my body.

# Proper Dates

We're going on dates now.
Like, proper dates.

But what's the point?

# DEEP GUILT

If Mămică and Tata
find out that I dating with Jess
their mercury hit sky high.

If family of Florica
finding out this,
they make sausages from me,
    put extra cash charge on Tata.

        Whole lots of shit
        hit
        fan.

I should to feel
in the deepest of
guilt
for being with Jess,
but
I don't.

I will never.

# Know Each Other Better

Terry's sitting on my bed
flicking through a battered copy of
*Matilda*.
He grins when I come in.

I'm not sure what he wants.

'All right?' he asks.

He closes the book,
     leans forward and
carefully puts it
     back on the shelf
between a scrapbook
and some old CDs
Liam gave me years ago.

'I've been thinking,' he says.
'You and me never do anything together.
We should start.
We should get to know each other better.'

I take an almost invisible step
back
into the hall.
'You've known me since I was eight, Terry,' I say,
as happily as I can.

He nods, stands, comes forward
                    and takes my hand
so he can pull me into the room,
then
uses a foot to kick the door closed.
'Yeah, I know that.
But when you're a teenager you change, don't you?
I've seen the changes in you.
I wanna get to know who you are now.'

He sits back down on the bed
and cos
he has my hand, I've got no choice but to
sit down too,
when what I really want to do
is run,
            get out of that room
as quick as I can.

But why am I suddenly so afraid?
Terry's never hit me.
He's never put me in one of his films.

'Maybe we could go swimming or something,' he
    says.
'Do you like swimming?'

'I suppose so.'

'Maybe you'd be shy in a bikini though.'

'I don't know, Terry.'

'Nah, it's hard to know how you'd feel
about that sort of thing until the
time comes.'

He pats my knee
then
goes to the door.
'We'll find something fun to do.
Just don't tell your mum.
You know what a sulk she is
when she thinks
we've ganged up against her.'

He closes the door.

I stare at it
and know only
one thing:

I have to get out of here.

# I SPY

At bus shelter
we hide from England rain.
Two people
too close
that we make connect with
shoulder and thigh.

Jess crush closer
like I am cosy cushion.

She cuddle tight
like she fear this rain too much.

She squeeze my arm
like priests hold bibles.

I thinking,
this body talk is not because of England weather.

So I try to cheer
with game she teach me.

I search.
      I looking.

I seeing,
one Ford car,

one flag of England
and
one flower shop.

    'Jess?' I say.
    'What?'
    'I spy with my little eye something beginning
    with . . . F.'

Jess don't do eye spying.
She look at feet.
    'Fucking family.'

I want to reaching her hand,
be her calm.
Because I knowing who she speak about.
    'You mean Terry?'

And she lift her
face from feet.

# The Things He Does

'See, he's not really a normal person.
He's an animal
and you can't tell when he's gonna bite.
Not that he ever fights with me.
Not, like, directly.'

Nicu listens
without looking shocked,
without interrupting,
without making me feel like
a freak.

'It's Mum who gets it.
You wouldn't believe the things he does
    to hurt her –
the punching and kicking –
and he makes me film everything
like he's making a bloody documentary.'

Now Nicu winces.
'I'm sorry,' he says,
and reaches for my hand.

# IN THE FEAR

When Jess tell me things
he do –
    *smacks Mum around*
    and
    *punches her black and blue*
    and
    *boots her like a football*
– I wanting to wrestle him hard.

Wrestle him to ground,
wrestle him to pain,

to pieces.

For Jess
Terry equal terror,
Terry equal terrible.

Jess should not be in this fear.

# Nothing Like Him

I don't tell Nicu
about Terry
sitting on my bed
and
offering to be my best mate
cos
I can't really explain
what it was
that made me so afraid.

Not in actual words.

And when Terry's out
and I try to tell Mum,
mumbling and getting confused
about exactly what he said,
she frowns and scratches her forehead
like I've asked her an impossible
*University Challenge* question.
'He said he wanted to take you swimming.
   So what?'

'So, it's weird, Mum.'

'Is it? He's like your dad, Jess.'

'No. No, he isn't like my dad.

He's nothing like Dad.
Dad wasn't a total prick.'

She sighs.
'He was to *me*,' she says.

'Mum . . .'

I can see she knows what I'm trying to say
but she doesn't really want to hear it.
She can't hear it
cos of what it'll mean
for both of us.

'If we keep our heads down, Jess . . .' she whispers.
'Look, he hasn't laid a hand on me for ages.'
She bites into a custard cream.
There's a yellow bruise on her forearm.

'You're never gonna leave, are you?'
I ask.

She stops chewing the biscuit,
blinks hard.
'We've nowhere to go,' she says.
'And even if we did . . .
          he'd find us.'

# STUPID THINGS

Tata say stupid things:

> 'You'll soon be the head of your own family.'
> 'A good wife should always make you feel strong
> in the stomach.'
> 'Only ten days to go.'

He point to **X** on calendar.

Mămică also say stupid things:

> 'She's so lucky to be getting someone like you,
>    Nicu.'
> 'A good wife should always make everything
>    happier.'
> 'Ten days will fly by.'

She point to **X** on calendar.

I hate this bloody calendar.

# An Idea

He sits next to me in detention
and pulls his chair really close.

He smells of salt and vinegar crisps.
The sleeves of his blazer are
   too short.

'What do you want?' I murmur.

But it isn't his fault everything looks like hell.
He's the only thing in my life
I even like.

Nicu stays where he is.
'Why you being not my mate
all of a suddenly?' he says.

Mr Tierney looks up,
points a red ballpoint pen at Nicu.
He didn't notice him walk in.
   'Who are *you*?' he asks.

'My name is Nicu.
P.E. teacher tell me I must to come
because I not have proper football shoes.'

'I've no idea what you're talking about,

but just sit down.
And sit away from *her*.'
Mr Tierney circles his pen in my direction
like a wand.

'You act like tough cookie.
But you not cookie,' Nicu says.

I can't help laughing.

Even when I'm fed up
he breaks me down
somehow.

Nicu takes the seat in front,
opens his bag and pulls out a book.

I stare at the back of his head,
his neck
brown and freckled,
his hair
hardly even brushed.

'Oi,' I whisper.

He turns.

'I've got an idea.'

# AT THE BACK GATES

So when she whisper
    'Oi'
I feel the blessing in my
bones.
Jess has the serious face on.
No smile,
no teeth,
no eye diamonds.
    'I've got an idea,' she say.
    'What idea?' I say.
    'I'll tell you after this crap,' she say.
    'OK.'
    'TURN AROUND, BOY!'
Teacher shouting at me.
        So tell me the new.

I stare at clock –
*tick-tock*.
It is longest twenty minutes
in life.

'Right, you can both beat it now.'
We sprinting to back gate.

'God, it's bloody Baltic.'
Jess cuddle her body.
But it not *too* cold.

I *know* cold.
When blood is frosty inside you.
When it hurting to walk.
When it better not to wash.

Jess blow
        little cigarette circles.
I try to pop them with my
        finger.
    'What is big idea, Jess?'
She does shuffle foot dance,
flicks fag
far in distance.

'What is idea?' I say.
'OK, you hate this school, right, Nicu?'
'In most times, yes,' I say.
'But you don't want to go back to where you came
    from
to marry some stupid girl
you've never met either, right?'
'Not in the chance.'
'Well, you're running out of time, Nicu. You've
    only got, like, a week.'
'Not week, Jess. Eight days.'
'And your dad's basically forcing you to do it.'
'He force.'
'Being a bit of a dick, if you ask me.'
'He is dick when talking of wife for me.'

'Well, that's just like me too, innit?'
'What?'
'My stepdad's an utter bastard.'
'You tell me before, Jess. And I sorry to listen.'
'And, this school . . . I can't stand it any more.'
'I understand.'
'That's why I think we should get out of here.'
'The school?' I say.
'No, not just the school,
        away from everything.
            you and me, Nicu.'


'You and me?'


'We could take a train somewhere.'
'Where somewhere?'
'I dunno. Warwick, Bristol, Glasgow?'
'This is idea?'
'Yeah, we should do it.'
'What?'
'Do a runner.'

*Do a runner?*

So me and Jess together for all the days?

Shitting sake!

# Madness

I mean,
he could turn out to be a Terry
once we're together all the time.
Maybe underneath that puppy dog face
there's a madman
bubbling with rage
and ready to do me in.

When I get home
my phone pings:

**I think yoor ideer
is most Einstein
ever. Ciao Nicu xx**

But that's the thing –
running away was all my idea.

So maybe,
actually,
I'm the one who's mad.

# CHAT TIME

'You need to wash your hair
and
put on these
clean clothes,' Mămică say.

My white shirt with big collar
is hanging on room door.
My fresh trousers
lie straight on my bed.

'You'll need a bath too,' Mămică say,
'The water's hot.'

Tata is silence.
His finger clicks at computer.
He get better and better
with tech work.

'Why? What's happening?' I ask.
'Tata has something he wants you to do.'
'And I need to wash my hair for it?'
'Don't be a smartarse, Nicu,' Tata say, his body
    swing to me on seat.
        'Just do what your mother says.'

I stare at them
like baby boy,
with teenage angst.

'Your dad wants you and Florica to meet,' Mămică
    say.
'He thought it would be a good idea
if you both had a nice chat
before next week.'

My angst go wilder
and
every organs inside me
skip a jump.

I thinking that maybe Florica,
any seconds,
will pop
from wardrobe
or
fly
through door.

'What? Now?' I say. 'She's coming *here*?'
'No,' Tata say. 'I've set up a Skype call for half seven.'

Mămică barber my hair
into Justin Bieber style,
but this not my look,
this
not me.

We wait for Skype music to
call us.

I wait to hearing Florica say,
    *Hi, Nicu, nice to finally meet you,*
but this girl is not my desiring.

*This*, all this,
is
not me.

# Packing

Terry knocks on my bedroom door
like a real gentleman,
        like someone you could trust.
Funny that,
cos
with the same knuckles
        he knocks Mum out.

Flat.

'Yeah?' I say.

He puts his head around the door.
'What you up to?' he asks.

I hold up a sock.
'Nothing. Just sorting some stuff out.'
What I don't tell him is that I'm packing,
getting out of here,
taking a train somewhere – anywhere – with Nicu,
and sticking two fingers up to him and
waving goodbye to life here.

On the bed I've got a pile of clothes:
trainers,
grey knickers,
jeans

and a hoodie.
Plus, every single thing I own that I might get a
    few
quid for:
a couple of old phones,
a hair straightener,
gold earrings Liam got me one Christmas.

'Where's your mum?' Terry asks.
His voice is sort of sing-songy,
chipper,
but I can tell from his twitching temples
he's about to explode.

'Dunno,' I tell him,
which is true.
I haven't seen her since yesterday.
She wasn't up when I left for school,
and the house was empty when I got home.
And cold.

My gut starts to flip.

Did she leave?
Did she clear off without me?
*Before* me?

'Can you see now why I get so mad with her?'
Terry asks.

His fist flexes.
Oh, God,
if Mum doesn't come back maybe I'll get it.
Maybe I'll be the one with a broken rib
and bruises where no one can see them.

'She probably went to Asda,' I say.

'Then why's her phone off?' he asks,
like I should know.

'Dunno,' I say again
and shrug.
'Want a cup of tea?'
I add,
because that's how Mum diverts him –
with food and drink,
and sex sometimes.

Keys rattle in the front door.
'Hello?'
It's her.
She hasn't left at all.
And I take a deep breath,
relief,
until Terry marches into the hall,
his feet hard on the floor.

I follow.

His fingers seize Mum's wrist
and he puts his face so close to hers
their noses touch.

And then,
very gently,
he presses his lips to her lips and kisses her.
He kisses
and kisses
and kisses.

'Shall we put a bottle of wine in the fridge
and watch a film tonight, love?'
he asks.

'Sure,' she whispers.

Terry turns to me.
'You still here?'

I squeeze my own hands into fists
and go back to my room to finish packing.

# RUNNERS

This what I thinking:
Jess is exact right,
it *is* time to do
a runner.
Runner from Mămică, Tata, Pata.

Runner from Florica.

It *is* time to
bugger off.

This what I also thinking:
I dream of
my heart
beating
on top of
Jess heart.
So we beat
like one.

# Not a Clue

In afternoon registration
I don't even look at my so-called mates.

I sit away from them,
at the back,
with my feet up on the desk,
and roll my eyes when Ms Allen calls my name.
  'Jessica *Clarke*,' she repeats, eye-balling me.

'Well, if you're looking right at me,
I must be here, Miss, innit?' I say.
I want her to notice me,
see I'm in school
and definitely *not* call my mum to tell her I'm
    bunking.

A few of my classmates snigger.
Ms Allen goes red and blotchy.
  'Do you want another detention, Jess. Is that it?'
    she asks.
She's a young teacher
who doesn't have a clue
about teenagers.
And small scuffles like this get her all hot and
    bothered.
I love watching it happen.

'I don't mind a detention,' I say and shrug.
She can do what she wants.
I won't be here at three-thirty anyway;
by the time the bell goes,
I'll be miles away.

With Nicu.

I leave registration and go straight out the
front gate.

Every other time I've bunked off
I've just headed to the park for cider
instead of going to science or whatever,
but today it's different.
I'm leaving.
For good.

I feel sick and dizzy,
so I go straight
to the corner shop to get a drink.

And then
I wait.

# CREEPING AROUND

Busy.
Busy.

Tata go out metal collecting
most days.
Mămică stay and do sausages, stews
and clothes.

Busy.
Busy.

So it good timing to become
ninja boy.
Creep around boy.
Bunk school boy.

Do a runner.

If they nabbing me in this act
I know
I'm the goner.

But
**X**
day
is getting
so closer.

Bloody wife!

The day Jess nerves
shatter
to end of her rope
is getting
so closer
too.

Bloody Terry!

Now is time for preparing
to do runner.
Now is not time for
delaying.

I go where Tata keep his
metal collecting cash.
His wife buying cash:
in bedroom,
top of wardrobe,
deep at back,
in box for shoes.

I lift box,
open,
and reach my hand inside.
Hand disappears in
tens

fives
fifties
oranges
blues
reds
      monies
      cover all my skin.

I stuff my bag with
all my needs.

I take much wedge
and
in bag
squeeze shove
it under
jeans and jumper.

My stomach do
churn spin
thinking if Tata catch me he do
left hook
      right hook
on it.

But I must to escape
**X**
day.

I must.

With bag on my back
I become the mouse,
           tipping toes
               on creaky floors.
I stop even from blinking
in case Mămică listen from kitchen
and know I not in school like usually.

I aching to hug her for last time
but
I fear to see the hurt in her eyes.
In eyes of Tata too
when they know
I not wanting
their life
for me.

And it vital important
I go to Jess
waiting
now.

# Batman

I'm outside Nandos
when I see him shuffling up the road,
a backpack over one shoulder.
He waves at me.

But . . .
        Oh, God.

He's wearing a cape.
Like a proper cape –
black and buttoned up at the neck.
Where the hell did he get it?
And
what exactly did he think I meant
by doing a runner?
Maybe he thinks we're gonna fight crime
instead of commit it.

Jesus.

'All right, Batman,' I say,
pulling on the cape's collar.

He frowns.
'Might get chilling at night, Jess,' he says.

'You look like you're about to go to a bloody

Dungeons and Dragons convention,' I tell him.
'Talk about conspicuous.'

'I not understand these words,' he says.
       'I ready for running though.'
He lifts up a foot, so I can see he's got his trainers
   on.

He's beaming
but I don't know what he's so happy about.
Does he even know what we're doing?
Does he get that we're not running
       *to* anything
       but
       running *away*
       with nowhere to go.

'Everything hunky dory,' he says,
twisting his arm around
and
patting his backpack.

'Don't say hunky dory,' I snap.

'Hunky dory proper English words,' he says.

'Well, coming out of your mouth
it sounds like bullcrap,' I say.
I'm being mean

but
I can't help it.
He doesn't seem to be taking this seriously and
I'm not running away with him
if all I'm gonna be doing is spending the next year
stopping him from sounding like a complete
    moron.

'How much pounds you have?' he asks.

I reach into the pocket of my blazer
and pull out a handful of tenners.
Nicu stares at the notes,
the Queen's superior face glaring at us.

'That all you find?' he asks.

'Well, what have you got,
Prince of Romania?'

He throws his backpack on the ground,
digs deep into it
and shows me.
'Where the hell did you get all that?'
        Wads of cash –
more money than I've seen in my life.

'It not good?' he asks.

'Good?
It's nuts, Nicu.
You *are* bloody Batman!'

He zips up the backpack
and puts his hands on his hips
like a real superhero.
'Glad I making you happy, Jess,'
is all he says.

# EYE BLINK

The guilt give me goosebump.

For cash in my pocket,
for destroying dreams of Mămică and Tata.
Also
for stealing Tata's
treasure coat,
the one he wear to village festivals.
But here is cold and chilling most of times,
raining and greying every day,
so
I needing
this
treasure coat for my own.

Jess make joke when
she see treasure coat first time
but that is OK
because
big part of her is piss-taker.

Her eyes wide open when I show my cash.
She tell me I am
superhero.
But I am greedy –
I want
*handsome, smart superhero*
AND

gentle kissing,
lip locking,
hand hugging.
Now, that would be
amazing.

We don't do any tender stuff.
No time.
We go quick
away.

But
it not so easy.
Sometimes London North
is too small enough
and we can't be
alone.

And we not alone
because everyone school bunk today.
Dan and his crew –
Punk Rock Hair,
Fat Belly
and
Neck Muscle –
bump us in street.

When seeing crew
Jess tight squeeze my arm.
  'Shit,' she say.

I feel all her finger press me.
Crew come close.
I pulling her stiff to me.
Body guard her.
    'Don't worry, Jess,' I say. 'I protect.'
My hand wrap around,
pressuring her waist.
I am Jess steel suit.
    'You not worry, I have you,' I say.
Crew come close.
    'No, you leave this to me, Nicu,' Jess say.

This is what I understanding:
    'All right, Jess?'
    'What you doing with that little thief?'
    'Where you going?'

This is what I also understanding:
    'Pikey twat.'
    'Immigrant wanker.'
    'Smack him.'

Crew do circle on me again,
so near
I smell the pong of booze and smoke.
    'Leave him alone, Dan,' Jess say in terror voice.
    'You stay out of this,' Dan say.
    'Slapper,' Fat Belly say.
    'Gyppo lover,' Punk Rock Hair say.

'Gyppo shagger more like,' Muscle Neck say.
Too many laughing.

People in street
seeing,
hearing,
witnessing,
but flick eyes on ground and
quick step past circle.

It just me and my Jess.
Alone on tiny Island.
With no person to
save us.

Dan flick Jess hair,
come close to her ear.
Very close.
Too close.
His mouth, her ear.
He make whisper.
Jess pull back.
    'Fuck off, Dan, will you?' she say.
Her hand squash me more harder.
    'Come on, Nicu.'

And we fast walk to small street,
away from crew,
away from whispers.

To leave the noise behind.

But Dan and crew don't to leave.
They follow.
Behind us in silence street.

We walk quicker.
They speed follow.
We stay in silent.
They don't quiet.
We don't run.
They move so fast to be in front of us.
All bodies stop.
I hear words I half understanding:
    'Plunge the prick.'
    'Yeah, go on, Dan.'
    'Right in his fucking eye.'

And this boy, Dan,
who
I have never did hurting to
ever,
listen to these wordings.
He listen well good
because
he pull sheen blade from behind jeans.

Jess does banshee scream.

I feel fire
and fear at same time.

Blade come to me fast rapid.
I dance
jerk back
slip slide
touch
tap
wrestling days back.

My hand go deep in Tata's treasure coat.
I feel for my Swiss Army,
*my* protect.

Shuffle feet
left
            right
reveal my *own* blade slash.

One
            two
like in movies.

The wild man take my body
to crazy land.
I see target,
hard advance,
charge,

arm straight,
lunge,
plunge.

My protect
rips
deep

in and
        out.

            And it sink softly.

Stab happen in an eye blink:
Dan falling,
crew frozen,
Jess calling
my name,
and
us

running . . .

        running . . .

            running . . .

# PART
# THREE

# Jess-Jess-Jess

I'm shouting and running,
and Nicu's
  behind me
shouting back,
and running too,
but I can't really hear what he's saying
except my name
– *Jess Jess Jess* –
over and over
like a bloody
siren.

# MR WOLF

Huffing
puffing
I hearing still his yell
inside my ears.

Huffing
puffing
I seeing still my Swiss Army,
one-two, in-out.

Its picture won't leave me.

I can't to breathe.

Eating air.

I can't to breathe.

Hurry
sprint
speed
lights of shops shoot past eyes,
blinding.

I can't to breathe.

# Blood on Our Hands

'What the *fuck* was that?'
I'm screaming
and Nicu's
   behind me
screaming back.

What just happened?
Did Dan get stabbed?

I mean,
*Wood-Green-gang-stabbed*
like the proper hood boy he pretends to be?
Yeah,
he deserved to get hurt,
but why did Nicu have to be the one to do it?
And why now,
just as we were getting away,
just when I thought things were looking
up?

We round a corner,
leg it down an alleyway
and almost collapse at
the end
of it,
hiding between a pair of wheelie bins.

'How badly did you hurt him?' I blurt out.
'Did you *kill* him?'

Nicu can't speak.
He's just gasping, panting,
then punching one of the wheelie bins to bits.
Punching and
hollering and
punching and
hollering.

I've no idea what he's saying.

'Stop!' I scream
and grab his hand.
'Your hand's bleeding,' I say,
feeling the blood's slipperiness between my fingers,
coughing up a little bubble of sick.

He exhales.
'Not my blood, Jess,' he says.

I close my eyes, thinking.

Thinking.

What do we do now?
Where do we go?
Mum? Dawn?

The police?
That's it:
we go to the police.

It was self-defence,
broad daylight.

I hold on to Nicu
tight,
two hands gripping his shoulders.
'We have to give ourselves up.'

'No.'

'If we run away
it'll look well suspicious.
They'll think we meant it.'

He shakes his head,
pulls his cloak
up to hide his face.

'We *have* to, Nicu.
We haven't got a choice.'

He steps away from me,
eyes filling with tears,
looking like a little kid.

'*You* have choice, Jess,
because police believing
white girl
speaking good English.
But me.
They seeing only
gypsy boy
with
criminal paper.'

He kicks the wall.

'Shit,' I say,
because he's right.
The police wouldn't believe him for a second,
and not just Nicu;
with my offender's record
they wouldn't believe me either.
We're textbook delinquents.
Guilty before we've even
opened our mouths.

'We must to go far away now,' he says.
'We can cutting hair and
changing names
and nobody remember
us
after.
OK, Jess?'

He wipes his hands on his cloak,
shudders when a dog in the distance
barks.

'Yes,' I say.
'I think we have to go
away like we planned.'
I take his hand.
I hold on tight.
'Let's get you cleaned up
first,' I say.
'Let's wash this blood off your hands.'

# SALTY SWIMMING POOLS

She pour the water bottle over my
blood hand.
I not hear what she say,
her tongue, mouth, words
all
happening too much fast.

Jess is angry,
in devastation,
totally pissed-off with me.

She is correct to be.

But
I want for her to give me
tight hug
and tell me
  everything going to be all right.

Instead
she do the big panic.

I try rub blood off my hand.
Again Dan's liquid
drop
one

two
on my shoe.

Blue and red lights
blur past,
and I thinking of Dan, poor guy,
and me without brain,
and why I always do the stupid thing.
Why?

What idiot idea
to using my protect.

And it come . . .

Like Falls of Niagara it come.
I can't to control
the tears.
My stomach and shoulders
bouncing
bouncing
bouncing
like the
*doof*
*doof*
*doof*
on the night of our
ice skate
date.

And I *still* can't to breathe.

'Come on, Nicu,' Jess say.
And she making her thumbs do car wiper on my
　　eyes.
'Jesus, don't cry.
It was self-defence.
I saw it.
There's CCTV cameras all over the place to prove
　　it.
I'm telling you, it was self-defence.'

Jess move closer.
Arms out.
We become one,
hugging.
She is warming.

Her touching help peace my mental
and my body.
'I only want to scare on him, Jess,' I say.
'I know you did.'
'It happen fast.'
'Exactly.'
'Maybe I make just little hole in him.'
'Whatever it was, we better get out of here.'
'Where?' I say.

The mobile phone shine light on
Jess face.

'Liam,' she say.

'Liam, is that you?'

# Clean Up

'Ok, see you later,' I say and close the phone.
I didn't tell Liam
why
I
so desperately
have to see him,
and I know he must think it's
something to do with Terry,
something to do with Mum.

In a way
it is
because if it weren't for Terry
I'd never have tried
to run away.
I'd never have been
in that place
with Nicu.

'My flat's not far,' I say.
'Let's go there first
and change
so we don't get clocked.
Quickly.'

I never knock on the front door,
but I do today,
to make sure Terry's not about.

Mum opens it and before she can talk out loud
I slam my hand against her mouth.
'Is he out?' I hiss.
She nods.
'Come on, Nicu.'
We slide past her into the hall.

'What's going on?' Mum asks.
She is staring at Nicu,
at his blood-spattered hands,
his face streaked with tears and sweat.

'Cape off. Trainers off,' I tell Nicu.
'And you have to change those trousers.
Mum, you got anything he can wear?
Anything Terry won't notice is gone?
When will he be back?
Did he say?
Is he out for the day?
Mum!'

She puts her hands over her eyes
and starts to cry.
'What's happened? What's going on?'
She takes Nicu by the arm.
'Who are *you*?' she screams,
like we've time for *her* hysterics.

'Help us or piss off,' I shout.

She runs to the kitchen and comes back
clutching a spray and cloth.
She picks up Nicu's trainers and starts to
wipe away the blood.
'I'll be back in a sec,'
I tell them
and dash into Mum's room,
where I rifle through Terry's stuff
until I find a pair of
tracksuit bottoms
and a T-shirt
that'll fit Nicu.

We might be OK,
I think.
We might get out of here,
get to Liam's place,
keep our heads low for a while
and finally make it out of London
where we'll be free,
all of this behind us,
all of this a stupid bad dream,
a new life.

Mum has finished wiping
Nicu's trainers
and he's just standing there,
sort of shaking,

staring into the distance,
being useless.

I click my fingers in front of his face.
'Stay cool,' I say. 'Don't go all weird.'
'OK,' he says. 'I try.'
I hold out the tracksuit bottoms.
'Go into the bathroom and
put those on.
You've got one minute.'

He nods and disappears.
The door clunks shut.

I bolt to my room
and pull out something completely
different to wear plus
a cap to cover my hair.
Mum has followed me in.
'What have you done?' she whispers.
'Oh, Jess, what the hell have you two done?'

I want to confide in her,
this woman who loves me more
than anyone in the world,
but before I can,
the room door rattles
and

Terry
is there,
standing and
watching us.

# OLD RED EYES

He stagger in hall.
I seeing
the red eye,
lip licking,
bull sniffing,
the predator animal ready to make kill,
this guy who does
trampoline on her mum.

'Who's this?' he say.

He zigzag to me
at bathroom door,
looking my body
up
down.
His finger goes below my
neck apple.

Prod.
Jab.
Stab.

'Why-the-fuck-are-you-wearing-my-stuff?' he
    asking.
'Terry, the boy's had . . .' Jess mum start.
'Was I asking you?' he scream at her.

'Nicu's my mate from school,' Jess say.

'Yes, I friend,' I say.

'We're just going out. We're in a bit of a hurry,' Jess say.

'I don't think so.' He growl.

Jess Mum try:

'They were just heading to . . .'

'Louise!' he bark. 'Stay out of this.'

All time he keeping finger and red eye on me.

'*Nicu?* What sort of name is that?'

'It is Romanian name,' I say.


After everything that happen

to me

now this.

This bastard man.

So close

he nearly kissing me.

His smell shoot into my nose

like poison.


'Well, there'll be no foreigners in this house.'

'We're just leaving,' Jess say.

'*He* is. You're not.'

'You don't tell me what to do,' Jess say.

'Wanna bet?'

'We go now,' I say.

'You better believe it kiddo,' Terry say.

   'But before you piss off back

to where you come from,
get those clothes off.'

He put big hand on my hip,
tug
and
yank
at my T-shirt.
'Get it *off*!' he shouting.
Jess shout, 'Leave him alone!'
And still he pull,
assault
and
attack.
But I no more have
my Swiss Army.

     Threw it in drain hole.

     I am protectless.

I hear sirens
in distance
outside.
*Nee naw*
*Nee naw*
Nee nawing
in my brain.

What to doing?
How to escaping?

His hand pressuring my neck.
'See you and your type –'
'Terry!' Jess mum scream more.

I seeing Jess body tight,
her mum face full of fright.

His pressuring gets stronger
until Jess grab his arm.

Sirens
screams
shouts
brain
pain.

Jess kick his knee with all her muscle.

In super slow motion
it happen.
Terry's hand
exit my neck
and
connect with eye of Jess.

Sirens

screams
lights
blue
red
      mist arrive.

I think to using my other self-defending.
Wrestling days again appear.

I escape from the hold,
then
advance my head with full force
and
connect with Terry's
nose.

Crack
break
bleed
fall
howl
and again we're

running . . .

      running . . .

            running . . .

# Understanding

'Come on, Jess,'
Nicu says,
dragging me down the
   stairwell
   so fast I think I might fall.

But even when we're halfway
down the street I can still hear Terry howling,
shouting over the balcony
every last bit of abuse
he can fit into his mouth and
hurl at us.

'We must to run quicker,'
Nicu says,
   tugging at my arm.

I make him
   stop
at the zebra crossing.

'Why did you hurt Terry?' I shout,
and then I punch his shoulder
again and again and again,
hoping it'll hurt *him* –
hoping it'll knock some sense into his head.

He looks like he might cry again
and it only makes me angrier.
I shove him hard,
almost
into an oncoming car.

We squat between two white vans
to get our breaths.
'He want to destroying us, Jess.'

'But, my mum,' I explain.
'*She'll* be the one who
gets it. Don't you understand?
Isn't there *anything* you understand?'

He holds my fists, so I won't hit him again
and presses his face up close to mine.
'I understand we have to run now.
I understand Terry is total bastard.
I understand I making your life
more terrible than before.
Tell me what I *not* understanding?'

Now I feel my own tears come.
And I hate it.

I hate crying
because that's not me
and that's not what we need right now.

We need to go,
get to Liam's
and figure out what we're going to do.

But we don't move.
I just stare at Nicu.
'No one ever stood up for me before,' I tell him.

He nods. 'You preferring I didn't do?'

'No,' I tell him.

'What you want us doing now, Jess?'

I take his chin between my fingers.

We come together.

# ON CLOUD TWENTY-NINE

When her lips touching mine
all
siren
and
screaming
noise

      stop.

It seem her kiss
sprinkle the magic
diamond dust
on my fear
and
my panic.

All of a suddenly
I'm in hot-air balloon.

Floating . . .
        floating . . .
far away
into different land.

I am in peace.

I am in
love.

When kiss ends
I returning
into the now.

Into

*here.*

U with Nicu? Call me.
Dan's at the North Mid.

Unde eşti?

Like WTAF U DOING?

Sunâ-ne acum. Poliţia îi la uşa

WHERE R U JESS?????

Te rog sună acasă Nicu

# No Junk

We can't get a bus
cos they've got cameras on them,
and in some taxis too,
and even along the high street
to stop gangs and muggers
and whatever,
so we walk
hand in hand,
quick as we can,
breathing hard,
thinking harder,
wishing it were different
and glad it isn't,
past the tube station,
all the way along Lordship Lane,
miles it feels like,
miles and miles,
until we get to Tottenham High Road
and walk up towards White Hart Lane,
the Spurs' ground,
Torrington Gardens,
Liam's estate,
and the red door to his flat,
which has a sign across it that reads,
*NO JUNK MAIL.*

# TEARS AND FEARS

Jess drop my hand
to *knock-knock*
soft
on red door.

When Liam open
I seeing his man face,
strong
like warrior Viking,
hair sea wave cool.

They have same eyes:
colour of sky
on sunshine days.

Liam look me once over,
same as Terry –
down
up.
His face tell me that he can't to see
past my
skin.
My foreign.
I want to say:
*Hello, Liam. Please to meet you.*
But no chance.
I look at my feet

and seeing Dan on my toes.
Still.

'Can we come in, Liam?' Jess say.
Liam step out of door and we step back.
'I can't help you, Jess.'
'But I thought . . .'
'I spoke to Mum.'
'Mum? When?'
'She called a few minutes ago.'
'Is she OK?' Jess say in the desperate.
'She's fine, she's with a friend.
Apparently
she bolted and left that arsehole
snorting on his own blood.'
Liam looking me with serious.
'Nice job, by the way,' he say.
'Where's Terry?' Jess say.
'Who gives a shit?'
'Liam, we need help.'
'There's no way. Leila will go nuts.'
Liam nod head to me.
'We'd be screwed if they nabbed *your mate* in here.'
'What do you mean?'
'Mum told me everything.'
'Mum doesn't know shit.'
'The police were at the estate, Jess.'
'And what?'
'Well, she sees blood on his hands and

both of you changed your clothes.'
'And what? Two and two make . . .'
'What? Big coincidence, is it?'

I looking at Jess.
We pressurise our hands to become one unity.

'What the hell will we do, Liam?'
'I can't help.' He step back inside red door.
'Please.'
'I'm sorry. I just can't.'
'Where will we go?' I hearing the shaky in her
   voice.
A volcano ready for the erupt.
'If I were you, I'd get out of London,' Liam say,
before closing door.

Slam.

Thud.

Lock.

# Action Plan

'Liam!' I shout through the letterbox.
'Liam, *please*!'

It's not like I thought we were gonna
*live*
with my brother.
I just thought that maybe Liam would know what
    to do,
that maybe he'd wanna help
after running out on me
like he did.
But he doesn't feel guilty about leaving.
He's taking care of himself
like he always has.

Like he should.

And
I'm on my own
again.

Except,
    I'm not
        alone at all.

My mind sprints.

We need an action plan.

'You've got money,' I tell Nicu.
'Tottenham Hale Station's not far.
We'll get a train from there.
Go anywhere that isn't London.
It's what we were gonna do anyway,
right?
That was always the plan anyway.
Right?'

He's staring at me,
or squinting,
trying to figure something out.

'What?' I ask. '*What?*'

'It OK to changing your mind,' Nicu says.
'You OK to calling police
and staying here with
family and friends and normal
life.
It me who make mistake, Jess.
Not you.'

I shake my head,
take his hand,
his nails still dirty from Dan's blood.
'You aren't leaving me,' I say.

# FOR EVER

'You aren't leaving me,' she say.

No.

I want never to leave Jess.

For
Ever.

# Lucky

A siren blares out somewhere close by
as a high speed train
        zips through the station.

God,
I wish we were on it,
wish we were heading for Stansted, then Spain,
somewhere so different
we'd hardly recognise ourselves
when we got there.

'Shit, there isn't another Cambridge train for forty
        minutes,'
I tell Nicu,
looking at the timetable,
my hood covering my face to hide it from
station staff.
'We should go somewhere quiet to wait.'

And we do.

We go outside
and find a bench by a burger van,
where we sit with our heads down,
thighs pressed against each other's,
sweating hands
holding on tight.

Everything disappears.

The cars and people,
the planes above and
the trains along the track.

It's just him and me.

All quiet.

And I think
for a second
how lucky I am
to have found him.
How lucky I am
that he came into my life.

'You not so worrying now, Jess,' he whispers.

'No,' I say.
'I'm not so worrying at all.'

# PLATFORM

'I need toilet,' I say.
'What? Now?' Jess say annoying.
'Yes, I needing now.'
'OK, go. Hurry up.'
'OK. Look after my stuff.'
'Fine. I'll meet you on the platform.'
'Platform. Yes.'
'Make sure no one sees you.'
I do little laughter.
   'I'm scrious, Nicu.
   I'm really serious.'
She soft touch my cheek
and look me eyes to eyes.
Hers say
*You are my heart*
without the speaking
and
I try to swallow massive lump in throat
because
we have sharing
heart.


'No kissing stranger blokes,' I say.
'Shut up and go,' Jess say and does
punching of arm
again.
She could be champion boxer if she want.

She could be
anything
if she want . . .
if I didn't make problem for her.

Anything she want . . .
if only without me.

# Time Sharing

Prison wouldn't be too bad
   if Nicu were there.


   If we shared a cell.
   Shared time.


I mean,
   he'd get on my nerves
   trying to tell stupid jokes
   or throw chat up lines at me
   which just wouldn't work with his English.


But he wouldn't hurt me,
   would he?


We'd be locked in,
   and locked up together
and he'd keep me safe,
   I reckon.


Prison wouldn't be that bad
   if Nicu were there.


But prisons don't work like that.


They aren't bloody love shacks.

And if we get caught
    I'm all on my own.

# MIRROR MAN

I look at my
phone:
many missing calls.

I look at Cambridge train time:
five minute.

I look at face in toilet mirror:
I want no more reparations
for self-defending against Dan.
How many jail years?
Five?
Ten?
Twenty?

I look my fingers in light.
Dan won't wash away
From them.
I scrubbing and scrubbing and scrubbing.
But still.

# I Can't See

He's been ages.
What can be taking so long?

The train approaches.

I can't see him.

The train pulls in.

On time.

I can't see Nicu.

# TEXTING

I can't to see my face in mirror.
My eyes are glass with wet.
A force is on my chest.
I am in wood worker's vice,
turning
tightening
twisting
tensing.

*PING!*

**Where R U? Train here. ♥**

I send text.

I arive now. C U on train. ♥

*PING!*

**OK! J X**

I remain looking in mirror.

Train leave in
three minute.

I can't to move.

317

Train leave in
two minute.

*PING!*

**I CANT C U.
R U ON TRAIN???????**

Phone tight in hand.

Train leave in
one minute.

*PING!*

**IM ON TRAIN...U???????**

My fingers shake.

My heart break.

Yes. Stay. I come to u. Ever ♥

I listen to train.
Doors beep-beeping.

Train leave in
zero minute.

I feel for the courageous

in my heart.
The brave decide
that I make.
Time to self-defending
Jess.

Engine is louder now.
Wheels squealing.
My heart is the wheels.

*PING!*
*PING!*
*PING!*

Time to set Jess
free
from
me.

And Nicu,
always stupid.

ALWAYS STUPID.

Plan to go on platform
after train has vanishing.

But
        train still there.

And I see her.

Jess

through door,
through window

and she see me.

Her eye
meet
my eye.

She see.
We see.

Train moving . . . and moving,
and we don't to
hold hand,
have kiss,
hug tighter.

We don't to say
goodbye.

*Goodbye, Jess,*
I whispering and waving.

*Goodbye
my Jess.*

# Train to Nowhere

'NICU!'
I shout,
much louder than I did when Liam turned his back
    on me.

'NICU!'
I bang the window,
kick the door,
so mad and so loud everyone in the carriage is
    staring,
not knowing
why I'm freaking out.

But it doesn't matter what I do,
       I can't open the door –
the button won't work,
even though I punch it and punch it and punch it.

And

the train is moving slowly,
leaving,
chugging up to Cambridge
without Nicu.

And he isn't doing anything to stop it.

He's just
watching me,
waving,
almost smiling
and crying too,
like a bloody big baby,
watching and waving,
sobbing,
and I know,
          then,
seeing the look he's giving me
that
there's no point
in texting him and
telling him to meet me in Cambridge
in a couple of hours
because he did this on purpose.

He let me leave.

'You *dickhead*!' I shout.
Doesn't he know how much worse everything is
     now?
He thinks I'm going to Cambridge, but I'm not,
          I'm going nowhere
and when I arrive he'll be
somewhere else –
on his way to prison probably.

'Why?' I ask,
but he doesn't hear me,
and I know the answer anyway.

I look for him but
the train is out of the station.

I am gone and
there's nothing else to do except
say his name
over and over in my head like a spell.
*Nicu, Nicu, Nicu, Nicu, Nicu.*

I sit,
stare down at his bag by my feet.
His cape is rolled up at the top.

I take it out
to cover myself in him –
his smell,
        his stupidity.

'Nicu,' I hear myself saying
and look into the bag again,
where I see
the cash –
        wads and wads of his dad's cash.

'You dickhead,' I say again,
and I can't help it:
    I smile.

# IN THE DISTANCE

I watch
Jess
go *clack-clack*
down
train line
track.

I see train disappear.
Two lights
wink at me
in long distance.

Everything now in long distance:

hands in mine
ice skate laughs
sweets on slide
running
hugs
lips
tears

every dream in long distance.

Life is all
*clickety clack.*

We come together.

Now

we come apart.

# BRIAN CONAGHAN

Brian Conaghan was born and raised in the Scottish town of Coatbridge but now lives in Dublin. He has a Master of Letters in Creative Writing from the University of Glasgow. For many years Brian worked as a teacher and taught in Scotland, Italy and Ireland. His novel *When Mr Dog Bites* was shortlisted for the 2015 Carnegie Medal, and *The Bombs That Brought Us Together* won the 2016 Costa Children's Book Award.

@BrianConaghan

# SARAH CROSSAN

Sarah Crossan has lived in Dublin, London and
New York, and now lives in Hertfordshire. She
graduated with a degree in Philosophy and
Literature before training as an English and Drama
teacher at Cambridge University. Sarah Crossan won
the 2016 Carnegie Medal, the YA Book Prize, the
CBI Irish Children's Book Award and many other
prizes for her novel, *One*.

sarahcrossan.com @SarahCrossan